"I'm sorry." Mica ~~...~~ **inadequate. "I'm** ~~...~~

Guilt gnawed at him. He'd ~~...~~
breakdown at the news of ~~...~~
get her safely away without any further delays.

She shook her head, sobs twisting her body. He clamped his teeth together, hands tight on the wheel. The sensible thing to do was to keep driving, get her home as swiftly as possible.

But he couldn't bear to watch her grieve without trying to comfort her. Maybe that wasn't the professional response, but it certainly was the human one.

"It's going to be all right," he whispered. Neither of them really believed that, but she needed to hear it right now.

A complicated mix of tenderness and protectiveness flowed through him. He shouldn't be doing this...shouldn't be caring about her.

But he didn't regret it for an instant.

Protecting the Witnesses:

New identities, looming danger and forever love in the Witness Protection Program.

Books by Marta Perry

Love Inspired Suspense

In the Enemy's Sights
Land's End
Tangled Memories
Season of Secrets
‡*Hide in Plain Sight*

‡*A Christmas to Die For*
‡*Buried Sins*
Final Justice
Twin Targets

‡*The Three Sisters Inn*

Love Inspired

A Father's Promise
Since You've Been Gone
Desperately Seeking Dad
The Doctor Next Door
Father Most Blessed
A Father's Place
**Hunter's Bride*
**A Mother's Wish*
**A Time To Forgive*
**Promise Forever*
Always in Her Heart
The Doctor's Christmas
True Devotion
†*Hero in Her Heart*

†*Unlikely Hero*
†*Hero Dad*
†*Her Only Hero*
†*Hearts Afire*
†*Restless Hearts*
†*A Soldier's Heart*
Mission: Motherhood
††*Twice in a Lifetime*
††*Heart of the Matter*

*Hometown Heroes
**Caldwell Kin
†The Flanagans
††The Bodine Family

MARTA PERRY

has written everything from Sunday School curricula to travel articles to magazine stories in more than twenty years of writing, but she feels she's found her writing home in the stories she writes for the Love Inspired lines.

Marta lives in rural Pennsylvania, but she and her husband spend part of each year at their second home in South Carolina. When she's not writing, she's probably visiting her children and her six beautiful grandchildren, traveling, gardening or relaxing with a good book.

Marta loves hearing from readers, and she'll write back with a signed bookmark and/or her brochure of Pennsylvania Dutch recipes. Write to her c/o Steeple Hill Books, 233 Broadway, Suite 1001, New York, NY 10279, e-mail her at marta@martaperry.com, or visit her on the Web at www.martaperry.com.

TWIN TARGETS
MARTA PERRY

Steeple
Hill®

Published by Steeple Hill Books™

Special thanks and acknowledgment to
Marta Perry for her contribution to the
Protecting the Witnesses miniseries.

STEEPLE HILL BOOKS

Steeple
Hill®

Recycling programs
for this product may
not exist in your area.

ISBN-13: 978-0-373-44377-2

TWIN TARGETS

Copyright © 2010 by Harlequin Books S.A.

www.SteepleHill.com

Printed in U.S.A.

Even though I walk through the valley of the shadow of death, I will fear no evil, for Thou are with me, Thy rod and Thy staff, they comfort me.

—*Psalms* 23:4

This story is dedicated to my Love Inspired Suspense sisters who worked with me on this project. And, as always, to Brian, with much love.

PROLOGUE

MEMO: TOP SECRET
To: FBI Organized Crime Division; U.S. Marshal's
     Office
From: Jackson McGraw, Special Agent, Chicago
       Field Office,
       Federal Bureau of Investigation
Date: January 3, 2010
Re: Martino Chicago crime family

An informant has come forward since the recent announcement that Salvatore Martino, notorious former head of the Martino crime family, is near death. The woman refuses to give her name or connection to the Martino family, but to this point her information has been extremely accurate.

The informant has thus far consented to speak only to Special Agent McGraw and is carefully concealing her identity. She is apparently between fifty and sixty, about five feet five inches tall, approximately 150 lbs. Her speech is educated and unaccented. Her motives and identity are unknown.

In her most recent conversation, she passed on a vague rumor that Vincent Martino, currently the acting head of the Martino family and his father's heir apparent, is planning an unknown, but probably bloody, tribute to his dying father. Please contact Agent McGraw with any information as to the woman's identity or the possible intent of this supposed tribute.

ONE

The woman's body lay on the cold, dirty concrete floor of the garage, a few feet from her car. She'd probably been trying to run to it when the murderer caught up with her. Her hands reached toward it, the right one smeared with dirt, in a silent, futile plea for help.

Deputy U.S. Marshal Micah McGraw forced down the sick feeling in his gut. A law enforcement professional couldn't get emotional about crime victims. He could imagine his police chief father saying the words. Or his big brother, the FBI agent. They wouldn't let anything as soft as emotion interfere with doing the job.

"Pity." The local police chief grunted the word, but it sounded perfunctory.

Natural enough. The chief hadn't known Ruby Maxwell, aka Ruby Summers. He hadn't been the agent charged with relocating her to this small, supposedly safe environment in a small village in western Montana. He didn't have to feel responsible for her death.

Bless her, Lord. Speed her soul's journey straight to Your hands.

The brief prayer helped to center him. Shoving aside all distracting thoughts, Micah leaned over the body, studying the wounds. One shot to the chest, a second to the head. Her killer wanted to be sure Ruby was dead.

"Her apartment was tossed, too. Might have been a robbery, but nothing's missing that we can tell."

"I'll have a look before I leave." He'd been in Ruby's apartment a couple of times when he'd come to check on her.

"This looks more like a professional hit than a robbery gone bad." Chief Burrows made it sound like a question.

"Yeah."

He knew only too well what was in the man's mind. What would a professional hit man be doing in the remote reaches of western Montana on a cold January night? Why would anyone want to kill this seemingly inoffensive woman who'd been waiting tables at the Village Café for the past year?

And most of all, what did the U.S. Marshals Service have to do with it?

All good questions. Unfortunately he couldn't answer any of them. Secrecy was the crucial element that made the Federal Witness Protection Program so successful. Breach that, and everything that had been gained in the battle against organized crime would be lost.

He straightened, brushing his hands together even though he hadn't touched anything. "My office will have a team here in a couple of hours. Until then—"

"Yeah, yeah, I know." Chief Burrows let annoyance show. "Cordon the scene, don't touch anything, don't say anything to anyone."

"That's about it. Sorry," he added.

He was sorry, though Burrows probably didn't believe it. Brownsville was the chief's town, and he was responsible for keeping the people in it safe. Burrows probably hadn't had a murder in this sleepy place in years, and now that there was one, the feds were brushing him aside.

Micah's father, a police chief in a Chicago suburb before his death, would have felt the same way about a crime on his turf.

His cell buzzed, and he turned away from the disgruntled chief to answer it. "McGraw."

"The crime scene team is on its way." The voice was that of Mac Sellers, a fellow marshal sidelined to desk duty after an injury. "Should be there in about an hour."

"Good. Make sure they know to check out the apartment, as well as the garage."

"Will do. You wanted the address for the woman's next of kin?"

"Right." Ruby had a twin sister, he knew. She'd have to be notified. Since she lived back east, at least he wouldn't be the one to do that.

"Jade Summers." Mac was probably reading from a computer screen. "Librarian. Current address is 45 Rock Lane, White Rock, Montana."

For an instant Micah froze, the cell phone pressed against his ear. "Are you sure of that?" He barked the words.

"Course I'm sure." Mac sounded offended. "I can look things up, as well as anyone."

Uttering an apology that probably didn't placate the man, Micah hung up, his mind buzzing with questions.

He turned to stare once more at the empty shell that had been Ruby Summers. She'd made mistakes in her life, plenty of them, but she'd done the right thing in the end when she'd testified against the Mob. She hadn't deserved to end up lifeless on a cold concrete floor.

As for her sister…

What exactly was an Easterner like Jade Summers doing in a small town in Montana? If there was an innocent reason, he couldn't think of it. That stretched the long arm of coincidence a bit too far.

Ruby must have tipped her twin sister off to her location. That was the only explanation, and the deed violated one of the major principles of witness protection.

Ruby had known the rules. Immediate family could be relocated with her. If they chose not to be, no contact was permitted—ever.

Ruby's twin had moved to Montana. He frowned. White Rock was probably forty miles or so east of Billings. Not exactly around the corner from her sister.

But the fact that she was in Montana had to mean that they'd been in contact. And that contact just might have led to Ruby's death.

He glanced at his watch. He'd have to wait until the team arrived and all the routine that followed a violent death rolled into motion. Then he'd get back on the road toward Billings and beyond, to White Rock. To find Jade Summers and get some answers.

Jade pulled a warm sweater over her head. After nearly a year in Montana, she'd learned to love the Big Sky Country, with its spectacular scenery, clean air and friendly, independent people.

But if she stayed her whole life, she'd probably never get used to the cold winters. Her indoor-outdoor thermometer declared that it was two below zero now, and the weather forecaster had cheerfully announced that it felt like sixteen below. The thought made her shiver even in her warm bedroom.

Still, the good things about the move far outweighed the bad. She had her own little house, neat and clean and everything she had once dreamed of. She could run the small county library to suit her ideas of what a library should be. She'd made friends here. She was settled.

Had Ruby adapted yet to life in Montana? Her twin had loved warmth—warmth, comfort, luxury. All the things their early life had denied them. Was she happy now with the way things had turned out?

Or was she pestering the Witness Protection Program to relocate her someplace warm? Jade had to smile at the thought of her sharp-tongued twin taking on some hapless U.S. Marshal.

The sound of a vehicle coming down her narrow lane caught her attention. That probably wasn't Herb or Ellen Trask, her landlords. Herb had been over at first light to plow her lane for her after last night's snow, and Ellen knew that Jade would be headed for work soon. Jade moved to the bedroom window and raised the shade.

A black-and-silver 4x4 stopped at the front porch. She was already learning to identify her neighbors by their trucks, but she didn't recognize this one. It was old but looked well-cared-for, like most of the trucks she saw out here. People knew that in bad weather their lives might depend on the reliability of their vehicles.

A man got out on the driver's side. He paused for a moment, staring at the house, and she looked down at him, her hand pressed against the cold pane. He was tall, she could tell that even from this angle. Beyond that, his jeans, boots, heavy parka and Stetson could belong to anyone.

He moved toward the front door, his stride that of

someone fairly young and agile. Definitely not Herb, whose paunch was visible even when he wore a down parka.

The stranger turned slightly, and the sunlight struck the object pinned to his jacket, making the metal glitter. A badge.

Jade's heart stopped for a second. Then it started thudding against her chest.

Ruby—it must be something to do with Ruby.

She raced down the stairs, feet keeping time to the violent beating of her heart. She hurried to the door and yanked it open while the man's hand was still raised to knock.

That faint shock in his brown eyes—was it because of her precipitous approach, or because he was looking at an identical replica of Ruby?

"Are you Jade Summers?" His voice was a deep, mellow baritone, roughened by some emotion.

She nodded, taking a step back, motioning him in. He stepped across the threshold, the movement bringing a wave of cold air into her cozy room.

He was even taller than she'd thought, with an air of authority that seemed to suck all the air out of the space around him. He removed his hat, holding it in one hand, revealing thick, glossy brown hair cut in a vaguely military manner.

He had a slash of straight dark brows, a lean, tanned face and a jaw that might have been carved from teak. A faint hint of sympathy in his brown eyes softened the harsh impression.

Sympathy? Or pity? Her eyes focused on the badge. U.S. Marshal. The U.S. Marshals ran the Witness Protection Program.

Nausea hit like a blow to her stomach. Something had happened to Ruby.

"I'm Deputy Marshal Micah McGraw." He held out some sort of identification.

She shook her head in denial of the news he undoubtedly carried. "Ruby..." Her voice failed.

"I'm sorry." His baritone deepened even more. "I'm afraid I have bad news."

She couldn't stand dancing around it. "Tell me. Just say it."

His eyes hardened at her tone. "Your sister, Ruby Maxwell, died last night."

Maxwell. That had been the name she'd taken when they'd relocated her out here after she'd testified. It didn't sound right.

"Died." She repeated the word. It was odd that no tears sprang to her eyes. Maybe because she couldn't picture Ruby—vital, eager, annoying Ruby—as anything so final as dead. She took a harsh breath. "You mean, killed, don't you? Murdered."

That would be the way it ended. That was the only thing that would bring a U.S. Marshal to her door.

"She was shot in her garage." He paused, as if editing what he was saying. "I'm sorry. She would have died instantly."

Was that supposed to comfort her? She opened her mouth to say something, but no words came. Instead her knees buckled.

She sensed him move. He guided her to the sofa, lowered her to a seat, steadying her with a hand on her elbow.

"Easy. Just take it easy. Take a deep breath."

She wanted to snap at him that deep breathing wasn't

going to help her, not when her twin would never breathe again.

Why, God? Why? The plea formed before she thought about it.

Why did she bother? Ruby had always said you couldn't rely on anyone else—certainly not God. Once she'd have argued the point, but in the past year she'd begun to think Ruby had it right. If God cared, why was her twin dead?

She sucked in air. She had to say something—had to make him stop hovering over her.

"Last night." She swallowed. "They say identical twins can sense it if something traumatic happens to one of them. I didn't feel a thing. But we've been apart so long."

"Have you?"

She gaped at him, not sure she'd heard correctly. He'd moved a step away, taken off his heavy jacket and tossed it on the back of the sofa. Now he sat, pulling the straight-backed chair up so that they were knee to knee.

"I—I don't know what you mean." She stammered the words, mind racing. Ruby had broken some rule, probably, in letting Jade know she was being sent to Montana. A vague need to protect her sister moved through Jade. "I haven't seen Ruby since she went into Witness Protection. You must know that."

His gaze probed, as if he looked for a chink in her armor. "You've corresponded with her. E-mailed, maybe."

"No." What was he getting at?

"What are you doing in Montana then, Ms. Summers? This is hardly normal stomping grounds for an Easterner like you."

She had control now. She wouldn't let him rattle her. "I can't think of any reason why that would be your business, Marshal McGraw."

"It wouldn't," he said. "Except that if Ruby broke the rules in order to bring you here, that might explain what happened to her."

For a second she stared into those stern brown eyes, feeling like a jackrabbit caught in the headlights of an oncoming pickup. Then a cleansing wave of anger washed through her.

"What are you saying? Are you accusing me of contributing to my sister's death?"

He looked as if he might respond, but before he could speak, she swept on. "How dare you? How dare you imply such a thing? Ruby testified in that Mob case because you people offered her a fresh start. You promised you'd protect her. You said no harm would come to her. You cited all kinds of statistics to prove she'd be safe. If anyone's responsible for my sister's death, it's you!"

McGraw rose, and for a second she thought he was threatening her. But he raised his palm, signaling her to silence.

She heard what he must have picked up first—the sound of a vehicle coming down the lane.

"Are you expecting someone?" The question was low and sharp.

"No." She got up, shaking off the atmosphere of fear he'd brought into her house with him. "It's probably a neighbor." She took a step toward the door. "I'll get—"

He caught her, pulling her against him, his hand going over her lips. Her first instinct was to struggle, but his grasp was protective, not menacing.

"Stay here." He whispered the words against her ear, his breath moving her hair. "I'll check."

Ridiculous, one part of her mind said. But some instinct kept her glued to the spot, watching as he moved silently to the window. Keeping to one side, he peered out cautiously.

Then his body stiffened, and his hand moved toward his gun.

Micah forced himself to remain motionless, assessing the odds. Two of them, both armed, with their weapons out in the open, obviously not fearing any interference in this isolated location. Even as he watched, one man signaled the other to go around the back of the small house, cutting off any retreat.

His hand was on his weapon. If he were alone…

But he wasn't. The woman had to be their target. His first priority was to protect her, and he only had seconds to make a decision.

He reached her in three quick strides, yanking out his cell as he did.

"A place to hide," he murmured the words as he punched in numbers. "Think."

To his surprise, she didn't argue. She touched his hand, guiding him to the stairs. They went up swiftly even as he identified himself and gave terse instructions to the local police dispatcher.

She led the way into a bedroom, across it, to a closet.

That was the first place they'd look. He shook his head, but even as he did so, she pushed clothes back to reveal a small door. Hidden at the end of the closet, it probably led into a storage space. Not great, but the best they could do.

The sound of the door being kicked open downstairs decided it. He shoved Jade through the small door, pulled clothes back into place to hide the opening, and slid in after her, closing the door.

Their hiding place was a narrow, confined space under the eaves, redolent of mothballs, the ceiling so low he had to stoop. He hoped she wasn't claustrophobic. They were close enough that he could feel her breath on his skin.

She had to be afraid, but she was handling it well, at least so far.

Another thud, another door kicked open. The second thug was in the back now. Kitchen, probably. If he'd seen the rest of the house, he'd have a better idea.

He heard their noisy progress through the downstairs. A mutter of voices came, and then one rang out loudly.

"I tell you they have to be here. His car's still there, isn't it? Check the cellar!"

Heavy feet on wooden floorboards, followed by the crash and tinkle of breaking glass.

Jade moved on a swift intake of breath. He put his palm over her lips again, holding her immobile against him, shaking his head in warning, not that she could see it in the darkness.

"They must be upstairs." The one who seemed to be in charge spoke. "Let's go."

Footsteps on the stairs muffled whatever response the other man made. Then his voice rang out, probably as they reached the top of the stairs.

"…maybe this isn't the right one, either. What do we do then?"

Jade stiffened, straining against him as the import of the words seeped in for her, as well as for him. The right one? What on earth did that mean?

Thought was cut off as the door to the bedroom crashed open. Micah shoved the woman behind him as best he could in the tiny space. He pointed his gun at the opening. He might not be able to take on both of them, but he could do some damage to the one who opened that door.

"I'm telling you, they musta got out the back before I got there. There's no place to hide in here."

"Check the closet anyway. I'll cover you."

Micah held his breath, steadying his gun hand, a silent, wordless prayer forming. This was it—another second, maybe two—

The faint cry of a siren, growing louder, mounted to a wail. He managed a breath. That had to be the sweetest sound he'd ever heard.

The gunmen reacted even faster than he did. Thuds marked their progress down the stairs, across the lower level, out the door. The car roared down the lane.

Jade moved, squirming around him as if to open the door. He caught her, holding her still until he heard the cop cars pull up below. Then he got out of the closet first, holstering his weapon, holding both hands in the air, his badge opened in one.

"Up here," he shouted when he heard them enter the house, having no desire to start downstairs until he was sure he wouldn't be met by a trigger-happy inexperienced kid. "Deputy U.S. Marshal Micah McGraw."

Two uniformed officers burst into the room, weapons focused on him. He stood perfectly still.

"Who'd you say you were?" The older man barked the question, gesturing to the younger, a tow-headed kid who didn't look old enough to be a cop. The kid edged up on him carefully and took the ID from his hand.

"Deputy U.S. Marshal Micah McGraw," he repeated patiently. "Two armed men broke in. Their car—"

"We saw it." The older man checked his identity card thoroughly, then nodded to him to put his hands down. "Already put out an APB." He tossed the ID back. "Sorry, Marshal."

"No sweat—I'd do the same in your place."

"What about Ms. Summers? She here when this went down?"

"She's here." He held the door open, and Jade crawled out of the closet.

"You okay, Ms. Summers?" The officer holstered his weapon.

"I'm fine." She stood, straightening her shoulders.

"All right, then." He shot a glance at Micah, as if waiting for an explanation.

There wasn't one he could give, not now. He'd have to call in, get his people here…

First, he had to make sure Jade Summers really was all right.

As if aware of his gaze on her, she raked her fingers through her shoulder-length red curls in an attempt to restore order. She dusted off her pant legs and looked up at him. Eyes green as glass in a pale, heart-shaped face seemed to measure him.

"Is it over?"

Was there an honest answer to that? He wasn't sure. Her likeness to Ruby shook him, and he tried to ignore the image of Ruby's lifeless body.

"For the moment," he said.

TWO

"Why don't you just come home with me?" Ellen Trask asked the question for the fourth or fifth time since she'd sat down in the kitchen with Jade. "I'll convince them it's okay."

Jade didn't doubt that. Ellen might look like a elderly kewpie doll with her gray curls and cheeks as round and shiny as apples, but she didn't take anything from anyone.

She'd already gone one round with a patrolman who'd tried to get her to leave. She had come out victorious. That seemed to have her geared up to take on anyone to protect the tenant she tended to mother.

"Thanks, but I'd better stay." She tried to manage a smile, but was sure it failed. "I'd rather be here, in case they want to talk to me again."

Ellen didn't argue. She just got up, her boot crunching on a bit of broken plate on the floor, and poured hot water from the steaming kettle into their tea mugs.

"I still don't see why they wouldn't let me sweep this floor." Ellen hadn't liked it when the patrolman had taken the broom from her hand with a warning not to disturb a crime scene. "What's a bit of shattered china going to tell them, I'd like to know?"

She didn't know, either, so she just shook her head, wrapping her fingers around the mug. But even its warmth couldn't penetrate the cold place inside her. Ruby, the twin sister who'd once felt like the other half of her, was dead. She didn't think she'd really absorbed it yet.

It didn't help that her cozy home no longer felt like her own. The living room, the upstairs, even the front yard thronged with various people in uniform, doing goodness knew what. Strangers had taken over her house, beginning the moment Micah McGraw came to her door, bringing with him that aura of menace and danger. If he'd never come near her...

Well, that was a stupid thought. They'd had to tell her that Ruby was dead. They'd had to admit they'd failed to protect her.

And now they'd brought Ruby's killers to her door. Another shiver went through her.

Ellen, probably seeing the involuntary movement, patted her hand. "It's an awful thing, those men breaking in, just awful. I never heard of the like in the whole time I've lived in this county. Things like that don't happen here."

That was what she'd thought, too. Apparently they'd both been wrong.

"What do you suppose they wanted?" Ellen fixed an inquiring gaze on Jade's face.

She didn't know what to say. Anything but the truth, she supposed. "I don't know."

She had to struggle to get the words out. Probably someone like Micah lied easily in his job, constantly dealing with people who weren't who they said they were. Falsehood didn't come so readily to her.

Ruby had lied all the time when they were younger. The unpleasant memory seemed disloyal, but it was true. Ruby had always said you might as well tell people what they wanted to hear. She hadn't seemed to realize that people had eventually come to distrust her.

Maybe because of that, Jade had tried always to tell the exact truth, no matter how much it hurt. But she couldn't tell Ellen, or anyone else, about Ruby.

Fortunately Ellen was off on a string of speculations of her own, coming up with one reason after another for the peculiar happenings. Jade could stop paying attention as long as she nodded once in a while. She could let her thoughts worry at the events of the past hour, trying to make sense of it all.

"Lucky for you that marshal happened to come along when he did."

"Yes, it was." Jerked back to attention, she tried to sound noncommittal. McGraw had saved her life. She couldn't deny that. On the other hand, he might have been the one to lead those men right to her.

The back door rattled. She jumped, tea sloshing onto the tabletop. Herb came in, with Micah McGraw looming behind him.

"We better get along home, Ellen." Herb always looked somewhat like an elderly bloodhound, and at the moment, the lines of his face had deepened. "The marshal here needs to talk to Jade."

Ellen's feathers ruffled instantly. "Not if Jade wants me to stay, marshal or no marshal."

Ellen's friendship warmed her. But she couldn't tell Ellen the truth, and obviously neither she nor McGraw wanted to talk in front of her.

"That's kind of you, but I'm fine. I can't thank you enough for coming." Her voice wobbled a little on the last word.

Ellen rose and swept her into a hug. "You call us anytime, day or night. Better yet, come stay with us tonight. Or at least come over for supper."

"I'll...I'll let you know."

She must be more shattered than she'd thought when such simple kindness brought her close to tears. She tried to stiffen her spine. Right now she needed time to collect herself, to mourn her sister, to restore order to her life. And to get rid of the authorities, in the form of the man who stood like a rock in her kitchen.

When the door closed behind Ellen and Herb, she slumped back into the chair. McGraw still stood, hands braced on the back of the chair opposite her, his gaze focused on her face.

"Are you okay?" He said the words as if he actually cared.

"I think so." She took a breath, weighing what to say. "I guess I owe you thanks for saving my life."

That didn't sound very gracious, but it was the best she could do right now. She didn't trust the man. How could she? He'd let her sister down. He'd brought danger to her home.

The chair scraped against the floor. He sat down across from her, planting his elbow on the table, making the pine surface instantly smaller. Obviously he wasn't just going to go away. That would be too simple.

"I'm sorry."

She looked up, startled, to meet his gaze. "Sorry?"

"For your sister's death. For your trouble." He made

a small, seemingly involuntary gesture with his hands, and his brown eyes darkened with what looked like genuine sorrow.

Her throat tightened. She wouldn't cry in front of him. She wouldn't. But it took all her strength to hold the tears back. "Thank you." Her voice was husky.

He let the silence stretch between them for a moment. Then… "You knew Ruby was in Montana."

For a moment his persistence angered her. But what was the point in keeping it secret? She couldn't protect Ruby now.

"I knew. She wasn't supposed to tell me, but she did."

"How? Did she call you? Write to you?" He leaned toward her, face intent.

She shook her head. "She let me know near the end of the trial. The FBI agents brought her to the library where I was working to say goodbye."

"They'd have stayed with her the whole time." His tone showed he doubted her.

"Ruby was an old hand at fooling people." She almost smiled at the thought. "She fiddled with one of the reference books on my desk while we talked. I didn't think anything of it. I'm sure the agents didn't, either. But afterward I found the slip of paper she'd stuck in it. Montana, it said. That's all."

"She was in touch again."

She looked at him, startled. "No. I told you. I never heard anything more from her."

Level brows lifted above stony brown eyes. "You expect me to believe that you quit your job and moved across the country on the basis of that one word." Flat with doubt, his voice challenged her.

Anger flared. "I don't know what to expect of you, Deputy Marshal McGraw, but that happens to be the truth."

He leaned back in the chair, putting a few more inches between them. Stared at her, his eyes dark and intense. Waited.

She waited, too. If he thought he was going to trick her into explaining an act she didn't quite understand herself, he'd wait a long time.

Finally he lifted an eyebrow again. "So. That's it? You just moved out here on a whim. You figured fate would bring you back in touch with your sister if you were in the same state?"

Pain twisted inside her. That was exactly what she'd thought. But it hadn't.

"If I thought that, then I was wrong, wasn't I? I didn't get to see her, and now she's dead."

You were supposed to protect her. She didn't say the words, but he was probably smart enough to know she was thinking them.

"Let's go over it again," he said. "Tell me exactly what happened when…"

The back door opened before he could finish. One of the uniformed men met McGraw's eyes, jerked his head toward the backyard.

McGraw rose. "I'll be back in a few minutes."

She made no move, watching as he left the room. Then reaction set in, and her hands trembled. She clasped them, pressing her palms together.

She couldn't let the man get to her like this. She was not at fault in what had happened, and she wouldn't let him make her feel like a criminal.

Shoving her chair back, she got to her feet, grasping

the table for a moment as if she were an old woman. Then she moved toward the living room door. Surely they were finished by now. Maybe she could straighten up in there.

She pushed the door open, stepped through and stopped. Stared. And caught her breath on a sob.

"Get anything more from her?" Arthur Phillips, Micah's immediate superior, blew out a breath on the frosty air, sending up a misty cloud.

"Not much." Micah shoved his hands in his pockets. "According to her, Ruby tipped her that she was being sent to Montana right under the noses of the agents who were guarding her. Says she moved out here but never heard from Ruby again."

"You believe she actually came here just on the chance she'd run into her sister?"

Micah considered. He'd been skeptical, too, but… "We might want to push some more on that, but it sounded genuine."

"Could be, I guess. They were identical twins, so I suppose the bond runs pretty deep." Phillips's cold blue eyes surveyed him. "Or she could be involved herself in the mess Ruby was in. That would account for the shooters coming after her."

Micah nodded slowly. "It still doesn't make much sense. Why did they need to kill both twins? And I told you what I heard the shooter say."

"'What if this isn't the right one, either?'" Phillips repeated the words that had been echoing in Micah's head for the past hour or so. "What did he mean? Why was Ruby not the right one? And if she wasn't…"

"Like I said, it doesn't make sense."

Phillips's scowl said he didn't like things that didn't make sense. "Whatever it means, the Summers woman needs both investigation and protection. You think you can talk her into moving somewhere safe?"

"I can try. She doesn't seem to trust us too much."

"Try hard. Convince her we're the good guys. I want to be sure she's safe and someplace where we can get our hands on her until we figure out what's going on."

Phillips's tone dismissed him. Nodding, Micah turned back to the house.

He'd said Jade didn't trust them, but as far as he could see, that mistrust was aimed straight at him personally. And he suspected Jade had a fierce stubborn streak behind her prim, soft exterior.

He pushed into the kitchen. She wasn't there, but a sound came from the living room beyond. He went through the room in a few quick strides.

Jade knelt over the remains of a curio shelf the shooters had knocked off the wall. Her shoulders shook and tears rained down her face.

"Are you all right?" As he neared, he saw that the shelf had contained a collection of crystal bells, shattered now beyond any hope of repair. "Careful. Don't cut yourself."

"I won't." She stood, keeping her face averted, probably not wanting him to see her cry.

"I'm sorry. I'm afraid they're a total loss. Were they a special memento?" The bells must mean something, to bring her to tears.

"No." Her voice turned cool as she swung to face him. "It's nothing. I'd just like to clean up in here, if you people are finished."

She made it sound as if they'd done the damage. Jade Summers must have steel in her backbone, to react as calmly as she had to the events of the morning.

She had been shaken but dry-eyed at the news of her sister's death. Now she wept over a few broken bells. He didn't have a clue to what went on inside her. His chief was letting him play a lone hand with the woman, and he had to do it right.

"Cleaning up will have to wait. I have a few more questions."

Her lips tightened. "I've already told you everything I know. Whoever led those men to my sister, it wasn't me."

"Then why did they come after you?" He shot the question at her.

She raked her fingers through deep red curls, clenching her hands for an instant as if pulling on her shoulder-length mop would clear her brain. "How would I know? You're the professional. You tell me."

"Maybe we should go to my office in Billings to have this discussion." It was a pretty safe bet that she didn't want to do that.

"I can't do that." Her voice went up. "I have to get to work."

"The library will exist without you for as long as necessary. But if you answer my questions here, it'll go faster."

"I told you I don't know anything that would help you."

"We don't know ourselves what will help at this point," he countered. "Humor me."

She shot him a look of active dislike, but then she shrugged, giving in. "What do you want to know? I've already told you that I haven't seen Ruby since that day at the library."

He wasn't sure he believed that, but he set it aside for the moment. "Had you been seeing a lot of her before that? Even before her case came up, I mean."

"No." She hesitated for a moment. Sometimes people did that when they were trying to fabricate a lie, but he thought she just didn't want to talk about it.

"I hadn't seen much of Ruby in quite a while." Her voice was slow, reluctant. "I don't know how much you know about our backgrounds—"

She stopped, maybe waiting for him to fill in the blanks.

"I know enough." It was all there in the records, and he'd been Ruby's contact.

Her lips pressed together for an instant. "Our father was out of the picture. Our mother was an alcoholic and an addict. Our childhood was a nightmare. All I ever wanted was to get out—to make something of myself so I never had to live like that again. Ruby…well, Ruby didn't agree."

"So you parted company, did you?" Truth to tell, he didn't see much of his half brother, either. Sometimes siblings just didn't have much to say to each other.

"Not exactly. I mean, we didn't have a fight or anything." Her gaze slid away from his, as if there was more to it than that. "Ruby found my life boring, I guess. And I found hers…" she searched for a word "…dangerous."

"You knew she was involved with a guy who was Mob-connected?"

"No, no." She pushed that away with both hands. "Is that what this is about? Did they kill her because she testified?"

"We don't know that yet."

"But that's what you think. What you were trying to protect her from by moving her here."

"That could be. So you're telling me you were living in the same city with your sister but you didn't know who she was seeing?"

"I wasn't living in the same city, not for most of that time. I went to work for the Baltimore County Library System after I got my degree. I only came back to Pittsburgh when that whole business about the trial came up. I thought Ruby might need me."

She was looking down at the shattered glass on the floor again, and her hands worked as if it caused her pain not to be able to clean it up.

Baltimore. That was something to look into, at least. If Jade had been that far away, it seemed unlikely that she could have been involved in anything having to do with the Mob in Pittsburgh.

They'd check on it. Just like they'd check on hundreds of other details. And in the meantime, the shooters were out there on the loose, maybe waiting for another crack at killing Jade.

"Is that all?" She glanced up at him, looking like a kid longing to hear that an ordeal was over.

Unfortunately he couldn't believe that hers was. "Not entirely. We'd like to move you to a safer location for a time. If you'll pack what you need—"

"No. I'm not going anywhere." That soft jaw managed to look amazingly stubborn. "This is my home."

"You're not safe here. Let us take care of you."

Anger flared in her eyes. "The way you took care of my sister?"

His fists clenched. "Those men could come back. Do you want to face them on your own?"

Her face whitened, but she didn't drop her gaze. They

stared at each other, wary as strange cats, and he felt the force of her determination pushing against him.

Footsteps thudded on the front porch, and the county sheriff came in, knocking snow off his boots.

"There you are, McGraw. We've got some good news for you. Looks like you're not going to have to worry about those two gunmen anymore."

"What do you mean?"

And why was he talking in front of a witness? Overweight, overage and out of shape, the man was obviously too full of his news to be discreet.

"I don't know where they were for the past couple hours, but a few minutes ago they tried to run a roadblock we'd set up out on the highway."

"You've got them?" Maybe now they'd get some answers.

"Well, not exactly." The man's pudgy face expressed disappointment. "Thing is, they tried to bust their way through the barrier, lost control of the vehicle, ended up wrapped around a utility pole. One's dead, the other's on his way to the hospital in critical condition."

And probably not able to talk, the way their luck was running. "You've got a guard on him?"

"Of course." The sheriff looked offended.

"That means I'm safe," Jade said, drawing his attention back to her. "There's no reason why I have to go."

All his instincts screamed at the thought of leaving her here alone, no matter what had happened to the shooters. "You'd still be safer in a hotel in Billings."

Her jaw set. "I'm staying here."

"Well, shoot, we'll look after Ms. Summers, Marshal. We think highly of her around here." The sheriff beamed.

"You federal boys don't need to think we can't take care of our own."

He'd argue, but he was on shaky ground. Jade could be right, and the threat to her could be over. The sheriff could be right, and he was capable of looking after her.

Could be. But he doubted it.

He looked at Jade and imagined her lying on a cold concrete floor with two bullet holes in her. His gut twisted.

He nodded. "I'll be in touch," he said. It was all he could do.

THREE

The briefing seemed to be stagnating, and Micah shifted restlessly in his chair. They'd gone over and over the little they knew about Ruby's murder, and it seemed to him they were no further.

Phillips tapped a pen on the tabletop, the only sign of frustration he allowed himself. "Mac, what's the scuttlebutt from Pittsburgh? Does the organized crime team there have anything?"

Mac Sellers straightened at being appealed to. Years behind a desk had softened his belly and soured his disposition, but he'd learned how to work the complicated threads that bound law enforcement agencies together, and that could be invaluable.

"Nothing that moves us forward. No indication that the Pittsburgh Mob was interested in sending any messages by tracking her down. Why would they? The guy she put away was a low-level soldier, easily replaced."

"What about him?" Phillips snapped. "He might be carrying a grudge."

"That's more promising." Mac seemed to like drawing out his moment of attention. "Joey Buffano, his name was. Seems Joey got himself a fancy lawyer, got his sentence reduced on some technicality or other."

A low murmur went around the table. Nobody liked the idea of a perp getting out early because somebody had slipped up.

"Anyway, they're looking into Joey for us, but the immediate word was that he's been doing an impression of a model citizen, working at his parents' meat market and reporting to his parole officer on schedule."

Phillips made a complicated sound that expressed doubt at Joey's turnaround and skepticism at his apparent alibi.

"Keep after them. The two we've got on ice were low-level muscle. Maybe they were doing Joey a favor." He looked around the table. "Anything else need following up on?"

Micah didn't particularly want to bring up this subject, but better it come from him than from someone else. "Yes. How did the shooters locate Jade Summers? And why did they bother coming after her?"

"I don't know why, but I can guess how." Mac sounded pleased that he had something to contribute. "I was going over the report from Ruby Maxwell's apartment. Inside her Bible they found a newspaper photo and article, announcing the appointment of Jade Summers as head of the White Rock Library."

"So they saw that when they tossed the apartment," Phillips said. "Maybe weren't sure they had the right twin, and went after the other one."

That meant he hadn't led them to her door, at least. "That must be it," he said. "There's still the matter of how they found Ruby."

Mac shook his head. "We could look 'til we're old and

gray and never know that for sure, but I'm betting she was in touch with one of her old friends. We all know that's usually what happens."

"We'll keep following up on it, in any event." Phillips sounded ready to be finished. "What are you working on right now, McGraw?"

"I'm still checking out Jade Summers's background."

Phillips closed the folder in front of him. "Have Mac help you with that. I want you to call your brother."

That jolted him to attention. "Why my brother?"

"He's the big expert on organized crime, isn't he? That memo he sent about the Martino family—well, on the surface it seems unlikely there's any connection, but he should be consulted. You call him." Phillips smiled thinly. "Do you good to stay in touch with your kin. All right, people, let's get moving on this."

Chairs scraped, fragments of conversation floated past his attention. He didn't heed them. *Call your brother.*

Okay, no reason not to give Jackson a call. It had been a while. Usually his information about his half brother was funneled through his mother. Jackson always maintained a good relationship with his stepmother.

Back at his desk he checked through the information that had come through in the past hour, looked again at the file on Ruby, and finally faced the fact that he was putting off the inevitable. And that he was probably being unfair to his brother. Just because Jackson's status with the Bureau was nearly legendary, it didn't follow that he looked down on his little brother's efforts.

It just felt that way. Between his father's reputation and his big brother's, there was way too much to live up to in the McGraw family.

He reached for the phone and called the Bureau's Chicago field office.

Special Agent McGraw was in. "Micah." Jackson's deep voice was crisp, as always when he was on duty, which was most of the time. "What's with a Mob hit in the wilds of Montana?"

"You know about that already." He wasn't surprised. Jackson kept himself informed about anything having to do with organized crime.

"I know about Ruby Maxwell. I didn't know you were involved, though."

"I'd settled her in Witness Protection. I was her contact." He didn't need to say more. Jackson would fill in the blanks.

"Rough. I hear you caught the shooters already."

Not me, he wanted to say. A county sheriff and a handy utility pole caught them.

"One's dead, the other one's not talking. The strange thing is that they immediately went after Ruby's twin sister, Jade Summers, who has no Mob connection in what seems a blameless life."

Jackson grunted. "Nobody's life is blameless. Does she know why they came after her?"

"Not that she's saying. We're keeping an eye on her, obviously. Even weirder, the shooters didn't seem to know for sure who they were after."

"It sounds like they weren't the brightest bulbs in the pack. What do you want from me?"

"There's no obvious connection with the Martino family, but my chief figured you'd want to know."

There was silence on the line for a moment, but he could hear the scratch of Jackson's pen. He had a quick, vivid image of Jackson in his fifth-floor office, looking out at the city that had been his home for most of his life—a life that he'd dedicated to eradicating the smear of Mob activity.

"Okay," Jackson said. "We'll look into it on this end. Keep me posted, right?"

"Right." He waited, wondering if his brother would say anything personal, not sure he wanted him to.

"Take care of yourself, kid." Jackson's voice was gruff. "Call your mother."

That brought a reluctant grin. "I do."

"Well, call more often. Stay in touch." He clicked off.

Micah hung up the receiver slowly, letting the smile fade from his face. Jackson hadn't said anything about the fact that someone under Micah's care had been killed. But it was a sure bet he'd been thinking it.

Stop trying to live up to a legend, he reminded himself. *You'll never do it.*

Micah McGraw had told her virtually nothing about her sister's death. Jade sat at the computer in the quiet of the county library, frowning at the screen. She wanted to look up details about the funeral service for Ruby, and she didn't even know where to start.

Would McGraw have told her more if their conversation hadn't been interrupted by those two hoods? Somehow she didn't think so. He was the epitome of a law enforcement professional. She'd been glad of that when he'd protected her during those terrifying moments she hadn't known if each breath would be her last.

But now that the fear had subsided, she found she resented everything about the man—his iron control, his snapped questions, his air of doubt at everything she'd said.

And most of all, she resented the fact that he'd left her completely in the dark about her sister's life and death. Where had Ruby been living during her time in Montana? What had she done? Had she made friends, enjoyed life, learned to laugh again? Or had she been living in fear?

The fear would have been justified.

She bit her lip. This was ridiculous. She was a librarian. She knew how to research. If the U.S. Marshal Service, in the person of Deputy Marshal McGraw, wouldn't confide in her the details of her own sister's death, she'd find out for herself.

Fingers flying, she started combing through the records of Montana newspapers. Somewhere there had to be something. Knowing the Witness Protection Program's passion for secrecy, they'd have clamped down on publicity, but they couldn't cover every base. Someone would be planning a funeral for Ruby, no matter what name they'd insisted she use.

Finally she found it. Ruby Maxwell. She leaned closer as if that would get her nearer to her sister.

There was no article about a murder, no hint that Ruby's death had been anything remarkable. Just a brief notice that funeral services would be held tomorrow at 11:00 a.m. at Christ Church, Brownsville, Montana.

She stared at the listing, her throat tight. Then she clicked on a site that would give her directions. It would be a long drive. She'd have to get an early start.

"Going somewhere?"

The words sent her spinning in her chair. Micah McGraw stood behind her, so close that her knees brushed his pant legs when her chair swiveled. She hadn't heard a thing to indicate that anyone was in the library. The man must move like a cat.

"I beg your pardon?" She tried to sound cool and collected, but her pulse skittered. If he knew she planned to attend her sister's funeral, she didn't doubt his reaction.

"I couldn't help but notice the Web site. You do realize that we need to know where you are at all…" His voice trailed off as he looked more closely at the directions on the screen.

Then he switched his gaze to her, his face uncomfortably close. "Brownsville. You told me you didn't know where your sister lived. Funny. I was actually on the verge of believing you."

She felt her cheeks warm. "I did not know where Ruby lived. I told you the truth."

He flicked a glance at the computer. "Then how did you find out about Brownsville?"

"I'm a librarian. I know how to do research. You people may have kept any report of Ruby's murder out of the papers, but you missed the funeral announcement."

"You had to know where to look."

She blew out an exasperated breath at his stubbornness and pushed her chair away from the desk. And away from him.

"Go ahead, check for yourself. Page back through my search. You'll see exactly how I got there. It took me over an hour to find the answer you could have given me in a minute if you weren't so wedded to your secrecy."

He didn't take her word for it. He leaned over the computer and hit the back arrow, flipping backward through the pages she'd searched on her way to finding out about Ruby's funeral.

Finally he stopped, apparently satisfied, eyeing her.

"Maybe I am wedded to secrecy, as you say. But you of all people ought to know how important it is."

"Ruby is dead." Her throat closed on the words, and she had to fight to say more. "It doesn't matter now who knows where she was."

"Maybe not." His tone softened. "I'm sorry. You could have asked me about the funeral."

"Would you have answered?"

That gave him pause. "I don't know." It sounded honest. "If my chief said it was okay, I would have. You deserve to know that."

Some of her annoyance at him drained away. "Thank you."

He jerked a nod toward the computer. "Those directions. You're not planning on going to the funeral, are you?"

"I am." She planted her hands on the arms of her chair, shoving it back as she stood. "I am going to my sister's funeral tomorrow."

"Jade…" He shook his head. It was the first time he'd called her by her first name, and it startled her. "You can't do that."

"Yes, I can. And I'm going to."

He glared, and she had the sense that he was counting to ten. "Stop and think about this. Ruby knew people in that town…people who had no idea she had a twin sister. If you walk in there cold, they're going to think she's come back from the dead."

Her heart winced at the words. She hadn't thought about that, and the idea added an extra layer of hurt. "I'm sorry about that, but it doesn't change my mind. Whether it makes people talk or not, I'm going to my sister's funeral."

"Have you forgotten that the shooters were after you, too?" His anger rushed toward her in waves. "It would be better to stay as far away as possible from your connection to Ruby. I'm sure my boss would say the same."

"Those men are out of commission now." She had to steady herself, because remembering was like revisiting a nightmare. "And they already knew about my connection to Ruby."

He frowned, those level brows drawn down over his dark eyes. "Even so, we ought to play it safe. We don't know why those two were after you. Or even why they were after Ruby."

"What *do* you know?" *And what, if anything, are you willing to tell me?* "Surely by this time you must have found out something."

A curtain seemed to draw across his eyes. "I can't discuss that with you."

"No, of course not." Anger lent strength to her words. "You don't want me to know a thing. You don't even want me to say goodbye to my sister." Her heart twisted. "Well, I'm going to Ruby's funeral, and the only way you can stop me is to arrest me."

His silence, lasted for the space of a long breath. And then...

"If that's how you want it."

"You..." Surely he wasn't really going to arrest her.

"If you're that determined to go, you'll go. But I'm going with you."

"I don't want you."

"I don't doubt that." His words held a determination

that told her arguing would do her no good at all. "But that's the offer. Either I go with you tomorrow, or I really will detain you."

She was astounded at the strength of her desire to throw something at him. She didn't do things like that. Ruby was the one who gave in to impulse, not her.

And if she did, he'd probably arrest her for assaulting a federal officer. Then she'd never get to the funeral.

"All right." She bit off the words. "Have it your way."

"I intend to," he said, and it was as much a threat as a promise.

The sun rose slowly, almost reluctantly, bathing miles of snowy emptiness with a cold, clear light. Jade glanced across the front seats of the truck at Micah. He'd picked her up in the predawn darkness, and they'd driven for miles without a word between them.

Her first impression of his vehicle had been right on target. The truck was an older model, but spotless inside.

Micah had shed his parka, revealing a woolly V-neck layered over a dress shirt and tie. The chocolate-brown of the sweater echoed the color of his eyes. He drove quickly and competently, managing the occasional patch of black ice or drifted snow without incident.

A twinge of guilt pricked her into breaking the silence. "You must have had to get up in the middle of the night."

He shrugged. "No big deal." He shot her a cautious look, as if wondering whether it was safe to talk after the way she'd responded to him yesterday. "I'm sorry for forcing my presence on you. I do know you'd rather be alone, but it might not be safe."

"Do you honestly think someone is after me?" Even

now, she found the events of the past few days incredible, still felt half convinced that she'd wake and discover it all a bizarre nightmare.

"Probably not, but it's better to take precautions."

She didn't know whether to be reassured by that or not. But he was wrong about one thing. "I know I didn't want you to come. But I'm glad I'm not alone today."

"There's not much anyone else can do when you're burying a loved one, but it's still better to have people around. When…" He let that trail off.

She twisted in the seat to see him better. "When what?"

He hesitated for a moment. "I was going to say that when my father died, I don't know how I'd have coped without my mother and brother."

She'd never known a father, but someone like Micah had probably had the sort of childhood she could only imagine. "How old were you?"

"Eighteen. My dad was a cop, killed in the line of duty."

"I'm sorry." That explained something about him. He was following in his father's footsteps, in a way.

She'd always been determined not to follow in her mother's.

He nodded, as if in acceptance of her sympathy. "And I'm sorry I wasn't able to tell you more about your sister. There really is a good reason for all the security. No one would testify against organized crime if they didn't think they'd be protected. And even then, it takes courage to do what your sister did."

Her throat knotted, and she had to clear it before she could speak. "I know. I was proud of her. Ruby was always the brave one when it came to dealing with things."

Things like their mother in a drunken rage, or a

landlord determined to evict them, or one of Mom's boyfriends trying to take money from her purse when she was passed out.

"What did you do when things got rough?"

"Hid, when I was small. When we were a little older, I'd get out of the apartment. I'd try to find someplace safe. That's how I first discovered the library. A whole building filled with books to escape into, and no one trying to chase me away."

A half-smile touched her lips at the memory of that first time, and Ms. Henderson showing her how to apply for a library card and introducing her to the wonders available just for the asking.

She'd never taken a book home, of course. That would have been asking to have it ruined or sold. Ms. Henderson had seemed to know that without a word being spoken.

Could someone like Micah possibly understand? If he did, that was almost worse than the alternative.

"Sorry." She folded her arms across her chest. "You're not interested in my past."

"Yes. I am." He reached for a pair of sunglasses tucked into the visor as the sunlight strengthened, sending up a white glare from the snow. "Ruby talked a little about her life, the times I saw her. There's no reason not to tell you that she seemed…well, content, I guess, with the way things turned out. She worked in a little café, made some friends, was active in her church."

"Church? Ruby?" She'd thought she was beyond surprises where her sister was concerned, but that did startle her.

He sent her a sidelong, questioning glance. "Ruby came to faith after she entered the program. I sensed that everything she'd been through had made her realize the importance of having Christ in her life."

Tears stung her eyes, and Jade blinked them away. "Once hearing that would have meant the world to me."

"Once?" The dark glasses masked his expression, but his voice probed for an answer.

She felt a little flare of anger. Was he judging her?

"Based on the way you talked about Ruby's faith, you seem to be a believer, but I don't understand how you can think God is in control with all the things you must see in your job."

Like Ruby's lifeless body, in her own garage.

"Those are the things that make me understand how much I need to listen for God's guidance."

"And when God is silent?" Grief put an edge on the words like a whetstone on a knife. "When He seems too far away to hear you cry?"

He took the glasses off so that she could see his eyes. They were dark with concern. One might almost imagine that he cared, but that was impossible. She was just a job to him.

"There have been times when I've thought God was pretty distant. I always seem to find that I'm the one who has moved, not God."

Unshed tears had a stranglehold on her throat. She had to struggle to force the words out, astounded that she was having this conversation with Micah, of all people.

"I wish I could believe that. I really do."

FOUR

Every one of Micah's senses was on high alert as he drew up to the small church where the services were to be held. He hadn't said too much to Jade, both because he hadn't wanted to alarm her and because it wouldn't be professional to do so. But he was concerned about her safety. There was too much they didn't know about this situation.

They hadn't seen the end of this yet. The two shooters might be out of action, but they certainly hadn't been acting on their own. Someone else was behind Ruby's murder and the attack on Jade...someone who pulled the strings and paid the money.

Jade leaned forward, hand on the dash, surveying the white clapboard building with its simple steeple as if she were looking for something. Maybe she was. Those few words they'd exchanged about faith had been revealing.

Be near her, Father. If You want to use me in some way to restore her faith in You, help me to be open to that.

"The parking lot is nearly full." She darted a questioning glance at him. "Curiosity seekers?"

"When we shut down publicity, we do it. No one knows that this is anything more than an unfortunate death." He pulled into one of the remaining spaces.

"Ruby was active in this church. She'd found a place here. It's natural that they'd mourn her passing."

She nodded, her lips pressed together. Trying to suppress emotion? He wasn't sure.

He climbed out and shrugged into his jacket, rounding the truck to join her. Together they walked across the cleared lot toward the red double doors of the sanctuary.

The church Ruby had attended sat a little distance from the rest of the town, giving him a clear view of the surroundings. He didn't see a hint of danger, unless someone was hiding behind one of the gravestones in the church's adjoining cemetery or among the mourners. Not likely since they probably all knew each other.

A navy blue canopy had been erected among the weathered stones, with a few folding chairs underneath it, facing the dark rectangle that was the grave. His gut tightened.

Jade sucked in a breath, and he put a supporting hand under her elbow. Maybe he should have tried harder to dissuade her from coming, but he could understand her need to be here. She had to say goodbye.

He pushed back a wave of sympathy. He couldn't let himself react emotionally. He had to stay alert for even the slightest thing out of place. Hurrying her up the single step to the doors, he pulled the right-hand one open and ushered her inside.

The organ played softly. The black-robed minister was in the act of stepping next to the bier when the door closed behind them with a bit more noise than he'd expected. Heads swiveled toward them, and the gasps from the congregants was loud enough to be heard over the organ music. Then even that stopped as the organist looked their way.

He tightened his grip on Jade's arm. This was exactly the reaction he'd hoped to avoid.

"Ruby?" Someone said the name on a rising note.

The pastor touched the white covering of the coffin, as if for reassurance. Then he strode quickly down the aisle toward them, holding out his hand.

"You must be Ruby's sister," he said, smoothly enough that Micah wondered whether he had known about Jade. "I'm Harry Davison, Ruby's pastor. I'm so sorry to have to meet you under these circumstances."

A rustle went through the congregation, but Micah sensed relief in it. So Ruby had a sister. Funny they hadn't known about that. That's what they'd be thinking, no doubt.

"I'm Jade Summers. I'm sorry if we're late." Her soft voice probably carried to the eagerly attentive people seated nearby.

Micah winced. He should have warned her not to announce her identity.

"Not at all, not at all." Pastor Davison was small, slight and balding, but he had a deep, resonant voice that must hold his congregation's rapt attention. "I'm sure you had a long trip." He turned to Micah, holding out his hand with an inquiring look.

"Micah McGraw." No reason to tell the pastor anything else about himself. He shook hands, wanting the amenities over with. He couldn't really relax until he'd gotten Jade safely home, but he'd feel a bit easier when she wasn't standing here like a target.

"Come and sit down front." The pastor waved them down the aisle.

Micah attempted to guide Jade to a seat near the door,

but she was already hurrying down the aisle in the pastor's wake. He had no choice but to follow her.

Finally they were settled, unfortunately in the very front pew. How was he supposed to keep an eye on the crowd from here? He leaned close to Jade, earning a startled look from her.

Too bad. She made less of a target with his arm draped across the pew behind her and his shoulder pressing hers.

The organist played again. The service began. The familiar promises from scripture echoed in his heart and threatened to distract him.

Forgive me, Father. I can't give myself up to worship when Jade's life is in my hands. I failed Ruby. I can't fail Jade.

Jade's fingers twisted together in her lap, and she didn't look at the draped coffin. Otherwise, she seemed composed. He wondered again what was in her heart, weighing that composure against her obvious need to attend the funeral. At a guess, anyone who really wanted to understand Jade Summers would have his work cut out for him.

Pastor Davison spoke briefly but meaningfully, reminding the congregants that they grieved someone who had come to them a stranger and become a valued friend and sister in Christ. He led them in a familiar hymn setting of the twenty-third Psalm to the accompaniment of the small organ.

E'en though I walk through death's dark vale, my heart shall fear no ill, and in God's house forevermore, my dwelling place shall be.

Despite Micah's watchfulness, he felt the peace of the promises fill his heart. He prayed that Jade took comfort from the words and from knowing that Ruby's troubled life had ended among people who loved her.

The final benediction was spoken. As they stood to follow the coffin from the sanctuary he kept a firm grasp on Jade's arm. This was a danger point, as people crowded in on them, expressing their condolences in the formal words people used to cover a wealth of emotion.

Jade managed to respond to each person who spoke to her, holding on to her composure. He wasn't sure how much that cost her.

As for him, he was too busy scanning the crowd, not knowing if these people were all the innocent bystanders they seemed. Could someone here have alerted the killers to Ruby's presence among them?

They moved through the door, fastening coats against the chilly air, donning sunglasses to fend off the glare of sun on snow. The pallbearers eased the coffin down the single step.

A middle-aged woman pushed through the crowd to clutch Jade's sleeve. "My dear, I'm so sorry for you. Ruby was such a sweetheart—always remembered how I liked my coffee, every time I went in the café. And always had a cheerful word and a smile. We'll miss her terribly."

"Thank you." Jade's voice reflected strain. "That's kind of you."

"Imagine her having a twin sister." The woman obviously wasn't the type to express her condolences and move on. "You could have knocked me over with a feather when you walked in. Just as alike as can be, you are. Not like that cousin of Ruby's—well, I guess of yours, too. He didn't look anything like you."

"Cousin?" Jade's voice trembled. "What…what do you mean?"

Micah drew her close to his side, his arm protectively around her. For the first time since they'd arrived, Jade seemed on the verge of losing her composure, and he knew why.

She and Ruby didn't have any cousins.

"It will be safer if we leave now." Micah knew frustration rasped his lowered voice as he stood next to Jade, watching the pallbearers maneuver the coffin along a shoveled path into the cemetery.

He'd drawn her apart from the other mourners. They probably thought he was comforting her, not arguing with her.

For a moment she wavered, her green eyes lost and confused. "I don't understand. What did that woman mean? We don't have any cousins." Her mouth twisted a little. "At least, not that I know about."

"Let's just get in the car." He tried to nudge her in that direction. "We can talk about it once we're away from here."

Jade didn't acknowledge his words. "You talked to her. What did she say?"

He let out a sigh of frustration. Short of picking Jade up and carrying her to the vehicle, he didn't have many choices. He had managed to stow Jade safely with the pastor for a few minutes so he could talk to Mrs. Calloway, the woman who'd mentioned this supposed cousin. He had her name and address for follow-up saying Jade wanted to stay in touch, but he doubted it was going to get them very far.

"She said that a man came into the café yesterday, asking about Ruby, saying he was a cousin. Mrs. Calloway told him that Ruby had died and gave him the information about the service. I guess she was surprised that he wasn't here today."

"It doesn't make sense. If he was involved with the men who killed Ruby, he'd know that she was dead. Why would he come looking for her?"

She was thinking again, the shock fading from her face.

"I don't know." There was way too much they didn't know about this case, and he couldn't investigate and protect Jade at the same time. "I promise you, we're going to look into it. Now, let's just leave."

"No." Her jaw set. "I'm not running away." She nodded toward the cemetery. "They're almost ready. We'd better go."

"Jade—"

She jerked her arm free of his restraining hand. "I'm going. Do what you want."

She set off, and he caught up with her in a few long strides. He took her arm, his grip tightening when she tried to pull away.

"All right, all right. But you'll stay close to me." He didn't make it an option.

She jerked a nod, and together they walked to the canopy.

The metal folding chairs were cold with an intensity that pierced through fabric to skin. The pastor must have realized that, as he kept the interment mercifully short. A final scripture, a final prayer, and then they stood together as the casket was lowered into the earth.

"The Lord is my Shepherd…" Pastor Davison began, and the others joined him in saying the familiar words.

Yea, though I walk through the valley of the shadow of death... Had Ruby remembered that the Lord was holding out His hand to her in that final moment?

Jade seemed to tremble, as if her legs wouldn't hold her up any longer. Micah clamped his arm around her as the final amen was said. The sooner they got out of here, the better.

"It's not going to take much more time to see Ruby's apartment." She understood Micah's urgency to get her away from Brownsville, but this might be her only chance to understand her sister's life, if not her death. "What harm can it do?"

"It's running an unnecessary risk." Micah sounded as if he was gritting his teeth. Still, he pulled up at the old home where Ruby's apartment was on the second floor. "Let's make it brief, okay?"

"Yes, of course," she said as she got out. She was getting what she wanted, so she'd try to be agreeable. "Pastor Davison said he'd make arrangements to have the apartment cleared and donate everything to charity, once I've taken anything I want to keep. And after all, it would look odd if I just left. I suppose if I weren't here your office would handle that."

"We would." He didn't sound convinced that this was a good idea, but he led the way up the narrow stairway. At the top, he held out his hand for the key.

"I can get it...."

He took the key Pastor Davison had provided out of her hand. "I'll go in first. Stay put."

The steel in his voice reminded her that danger might still exist, even here. She nodded, standing pressed against the wall while he unlocked the door, eased it open and then disappeared inside.

"Okay, come in." He held the door for her. "It's been searched, both by the shooters and by the crime scene team. They tried to put things to rights afterward. There's no way of knowing if anything is missing."

Her stomach clenched. She walked into the rooms where Ruby had spent the last months of her life.

The apartment was small and old-fashioned, but Ruby must have made an effort to brighten it up. She'd put a bright quilt on the sagging sofa and hung prints of Montana scenes on the walls. The kitchen was in one end of the living room, and the table against the window must have been Ruby's dining room.

"There's not much to it." Micah opened the door on the opposite side of the room. "The bedroom and bath are through here."

A framed photo of a group of women sat on one of the end tables. She picked it up. They were posed around a Christmas tree, and Ruby was reaching up to put an ornament in place, her face relaxed and smiling.

Her throat tightened. Ruby had enjoyed that moment. She looked younger than Jade remembered her, with her usual air of bored cynicism gone.

There wasn't much else to see in the living room. No books, but then, Ruby never had been a reader.

"Anything personal is probably in the bedroom." Micah seemed to be reading her thoughts.

"Right." She wouldn't be a coward about it. She went quickly into the bedroom.

The closet and dresser contained only the things anyone would expect to find. The only surprise was that

Ruby's taste in clothes had undergone a change. Gone were the flashy outfits, miniscule skirts and high-heeled boots. She'd apparently switched to jeans and sweaters, with a few pairs of good slacks and jackets.

She turned slowly to face the bed. Things that meant the most to someone would usually be there, in the nightstand, and she was oddly reluctant to approach.

She forced her feet to move. The nightstand was topped with a few books. She'd have to revise her opinion. Maybe Ruby had learned to enjoy books in recent years. She picked them up.

A devotional guide, a women's Bible study book. A Bible.

"Jade." Micah had approached while she'd stood there staring at the books. "I understand there's something in Ruby's Bible that affects you."

She glanced up, to find his brown eyes filled with sympathy. Then she opened the Bible and unfolded the newspaper clipping that lay inside the front cover.

Her own face stared up at her. It was the article that had appeared in the paper when she'd taken up her appointment to the county library. She stared at it blankly.

"How...how would Ruby get this? It was in the Billings paper."

"Maybe she'd been looking." His voice was very gentle. "After she let you know where she was going, she could have been tracing your whereabouts pretty easily on the Internet. You weren't trying to hide."

"She knew where I was." The words came out in a whisper, because her throat was too tight to allow for anything else. "She kept this."

The enormity of her loss hit her then. She'd never see

Ruby again. Never be able to say she was sorry for the lost years, for the pain that lay between them. For the times when she might have led Ruby away from her destructive life and hadn't.

"Maybe she intended to get in touch directly, once she was satisfied that it was safe. She wouldn't have wanted to put you in danger."

She heard his words, even understood them, but it was as if he spoke from a great distance.

"She's gone," she said, grief ripping through her. "She's gone."

FIVE

She'd had all she could take. If Micah had doubted the depth of her feeling for her sister, he couldn't doubt it now.

"Come on. There's nothing more for you here."

Holding her firmly, he guided her to the door. She didn't argue, didn't resist. He was taking advantage of her grief to get her out of here. To get his own way. What did that make him?

A marshal, doing his job, like any other law enforcement professional would. It was his responsibility to keep her safe, and the safest place for her right now was anywhere away from Ruby's life and death.

Jade wouldn't let go of the Bible and other books, so he took them, too, tucking them under his arm as he piloted her out of the apartment. If he was any judge, she wasn't going to hang on to her control much longer.

He locked the door and pocketed the key, then turned to her. She leaned against the wall, her eyes closed, her face dead-white.

"It'll be okay." Meaningless words, but he had to say something. He took her arm and led her down the stairs and out into the parking lot.

She seemed to rouse a little when the cold air hit her. "The books…"

"I have them for you." He got her into the vehicle and put them on her lap. "There you are. Just relax, now. There's nothing else you can do here."

Nothing else she, or anyone, could do for Ruby. Whatever guilt and regret she felt, he shared. He climbed in the driver's side and started the engine.

"I'll take you home. You've had enough for one day."

She nodded, her lips pressed tightly together, her eyes clouded. She clasped the books on her lap as if they were a precious cargo.

He threaded his way back through the winding streets of the small town, headed for the highway. He watched the rearview mirror as he went, alert for anyone following them. Nothing.

Still, that supposed cousin had been in Brownsville not much more than twenty-four hours earlier. He could still be around, even if he hadn't openly attended the funeral.

He didn't know what the man's purpose was, but it didn't take a genius to figure out that most likely, it wasn't anything good.

They could have the local cops question Mrs. Calloway again, maybe get a better description of the man. The locals would rouse less talk than sending a team of marshals in.

Flipping open the cell phone, he put in a call to the office and described the situation briefly, setting things in motion. This could just be one of those odd coincidences that turned up in every case, seemingly meant to convince the investigator of the randomness of events.

Or it could be important. He wasn't taking any chances.

When he'd finished the call, he ventured another glance at Jade, hoping to see her recovered. But she was huddled into the corner against the door, hand over her mouth, obviously trying hard to stifle her sobs.

"I'm sorry." The words were pitifully inadequate. "I'm so sorry for your loss."

Guilt gnawed at him. He'd been relieved that her breakdown enabled him to get her safely away without any further delays. That wasn't much of a Christian response, was it?

She shook her head, sobs twisting her body. He clamped his teeth together, hands tight on the wheel. The sensible thing to do was to keep driving, get her home as swiftly as possible.

But he couldn't bear to watch her grieve without trying to comfort her. Maybe that wasn't the professional response, but it certainly was the human one.

Snowplows had widened a space near a row of metal mailboxes that must serve the dwellings out of sight down a narrow country lane. He pulled over, put the gearshift in Park, and drew Jade close to him.

He half expected her to pull away, but she didn't. Maybe her grief was too deep for her to realize anything other than the need for comfort. She turned her face into his shoulder and let her tears flow.

He stroked her hair, murmuring the kinds of soft phrases his mother had used when he was small.

It's going to be all right. Neither of them really believed that, but she needed to hear it right now.

Her hair was soft against his cheek, and a complicated mix of tenderness and protectiveness flowed through him.

He shouldn't be doing this…shouldn't be touching her, shouldn't be caring about her.

But he didn't regret it for an instant.

Jade cried until no more tears would come. She hadn't realized it was possible to weep so much—for Ruby, for the years they'd lost, and even for herself, that she'd have to go on without her twin.

Involuntary spasms shook her, and her eyes were hot and swollen. She was aware of that first. Then, slowly, she realized that her cheek was pressed against the soft wool of Micah's sweater. His arms wrapped around her securely. Comforting her. She felt the steady beat of his heart.

His hand moved, stroking her hair. "It's going to be all right," he murmured.

It took a massive effort to draw away from all that warmth and support. Slowly, reluctantly, she drew back. Her gaze focused on his face.

All that iron control, that professional facade, had been stripped away, showing her the caring, gentle man he really was.

She put her hands to her wet, hot cheeks, embarrassment making them even hotter. "I'm sorry." Her voice was thick. "I didn't mean to cry all over you."

"It's okay." His voice was husky. "You haven't had much space for grieving in the past few days. It can be cleansing to cry it all out."

She drew in a shaky breath. Maybe he was right. She felt drained, but better. Emptier, somehow. Realizing that his arm still encircled her, she slid back into her own seat.

He dropped his arm instantly, reaching instead for a water bottle and holding it out to her. "Here. Maybe you'd better rehydrate."

"I guess I should." She took a long gulp of the cold water, wishing she could splash it on her face. "I didn't know I had that many tears in me. Ruby and I—we led separate lives for so long."

He handed her a fistful of tissues from a box behind the seat. "I don't have a twin, just a much older half brother. But I'd guess the bond runs pretty deep, no matter how far apart you are."

"Yes, I guess it does." Her memory slid back through the years, back to the earliest times, before they'd drifted apart. "She was there as long as I can remember. She was the last person I saw when I fell asleep at night and the first one I saw when I woke up in the morning."

No matter what the dump had been like that they'd lived in, she'd always been able to count on that. She and Ruby would have been together, even if they had to sleep on a blanket on the floor.

"Those early memories are the ones we always come back to, in the end. They're the ones that matter."

"Are you a psychologist, as well as a marshal?"

"Just someone who's experienced loss."

She managed a watery smile. "I'd rather think of those days. Bad as they were, things got worse later." She sucked in a breath, trying to still the leftover sobs. "Maybe the truth is that I separated myself from Ruby in my need to get away."

His fingers closed over hers in a reassuring grip. "You did what you had to. It took a lot of courage and determination to get where you are now."

"Not courage," she said quickly. "I told you. Ruby had all the courage."

He turned in the seat a little, leaning against the door

to watch her. "There are different kinds of courage. You made something of yourself against terrible odds."

"I had help." She'd never have done it on her own. "There was a librarian who took an interest in me. And a woman who ran an inner-city mission. They had absolutely nothing in common, except me. Together, they were a formidable pair."

"You still had to do the work. And I'm sure they wouldn't have put themselves out for you if you hadn't shown you had it in you to succeed."

What had they seen in her, those two strong women? Had they just recognized her desperation or something more?

"Ms. Henderson badgered everyone she knew to give me jobs where I could have a safe place to study as soon as I was old enough. She must have searched every scholarship program in the country to find the funding so I could go to college. And Sister Sally…" She couldn't think of the woman they'd all called Sister Sally without a lump in her throat. "Sister Sally taught us self-defense and Christ, sometimes in equal measures."

"What happened to them?"

The lump was back in her throat, but she couldn't cry any more. "Sister Sally opened her door to one too many addicts. She was killed for the few dollars she had in the mission box—dollars she'd have spent on people who needed it, instead of herself."

"I'm sorry. Did they get the perp?" His voice deepened on the words. Probably, like the law officer he was, he wanted to see justice done.

"Yes. But that didn't do her any good." She shook her head. "Sorry. I didn't mean to snap. I'm sure she forgave him the instant it was done. That's who she was. Tough, strict, but with a heart for any kid who was hurting."

"And Ms. Henderson?"

"She came to graduation when I received my degree in library science. She was retired to Florida by then, but she wouldn't miss that. We still talk often."

She should call her. Tell her about Ruby. Or at least, tell her as much as she could.

"So she's why you became a librarian." Micah sounded satisfied at having one piece of her history organized.

"She's certainly the kind of librarian I want to be…the sort of person who is a resource to her whole community. Not the stereotypical old maid with glasses and her hair in a bun, saying 'Shh' all the time."

He chuckled, reaching out to touch the wild tangle of her hair. "I don't think you'd ever be that."

She smiled back at him, the smile lingering for a moment, like his hand on her hair, and then fading. "Thank you, Micah. I don't…I don't know how I'd have gotten through today without you."

"You're welcome." His gaze warmed, and the back of his fingers touched her cheek, heating her skin.

She couldn't seem to catch her breath. She could only look at him, seeing the awareness in his eyes that must surely be written in hers, too. There was no sound, but she imagined she could feel the beating of his heart, as she had when she'd been in his arms.

He drew his hand away slowly, and it seemed to take an effort for him to turn, looking at the road ahead. He cleared his throat. "I guess we should get going."

"Yes." Her voice didn't sound natural to her. "We have a long drive."

And every mile of it, she'd be denying to herself that she felt anything at all for him.

The background checks on Jade Summers had come through promptly. Micah sat at his desk the next day, scanning them carefully, aware as he did so of how much Jade would hate having her life laid out that way for him to see.

She was a private person, very different in that respect from her twin. Even when life was beating her down, Ruby had remained outgoing and feisty. Maybe that had been her defense against the world that hadn't given her much of a fair start.

Jade had reacted to that same beginning by turning inward, taking her refuge in books. He'd guess she trusted rarely, if ever.

That made her breakdown in his presence all the more remarkable. Today she was probably regretting that bitterly. He'd guess the next time they met she'd be at her iciest, in order to deny those moments when she'd wept in his arms.

And what about that other moment, when he'd touched her and they'd seemed to see into each other's souls? What did she do with that? More to the point, what did he do with it?

He didn't need anyone to tell him the answer to that one. It would be professional suicide to get involved with a woman who was part of an active investigation, whether she was perpetrator, victim or innocent witness. So the only thing he could do was to shut down his feelings.

Too bad he wasn't better at that. He ought to take an example from his big brother. As far as he could see, Jackson had been shutting down his feelings for most of his life.

He closed the file on Jade and opened the much more cursory report on Edie Summers, mother of the twins. Just as he was telling himself that there was no earthly reason to waste time looking that far back in their lives, he saw one.

He let out a low whistle. Edie had been involved for a time with a low-level soldier from the same crime family her daughter later testified against.

Did it mean anything? He did some rapid mental calculations. The twins would have been about twelve at the time, certainly old enough to remember Georgie Messina.

He couldn't see how it fit in, but he couldn't ignore it, either. He'd have to talk with Jade—

"Hey, Micah." Mac Sellers rounded the corner by his desk. "Somebody here you need to talk to."

Micah's brows lifted in a question. "Who? Something to do with the case I'm working?"

"Nah. Probably just a crank, but the woman says she needs to talk to someone in Witness Protection." Mac ran a beefy hand over his graying brush cut. "I'm too busy to deal with it."

A flicker of impatience went through him. There was no obvious reason why the woman should be funneled to him, but Mac was prickly about handling anything he considered a waste of his valuable time.

Micah bit back a sharp rejoinder, reminding himself that Mac's ill humor had its roots in the injury that had robbed him of an active career and consigned him to desk duty.

"All right. Send her back." He closed the file and

leaned back in his chair, preparing to cope with another nervous citizen who thought her next-door neighbor was a Mafia hit man.

But the woman who approached him didn't fit the usual profile of the cranks who came in with odd complaints. Young, for one thing—probably in her early twenties, with soft hair curving around a gentle, sweet face. She hesitated for a moment, and then held out her hand as he rose.

"Marshal McGraw? I'm Kristin Perry. Thank you for seeing me."

"Not at all." He waved her to the chair next to his desk and sat down again, resolutely pushing thoughts of Jade to the back of his mind to be dealt with later. "What can we do for you, Ms. Perry?"

She sat, clasping her hands in her lap like a well-trained child. "It's a bit difficult to explain. You see, my parents died not long ago."

"I'm sorry for your loss." If she declared they'd been killed by a Mafia hit man, he'd start banging his head on the desk.

"Thank you. Well, it was very sudden, and I had to take care of all my parents' papers and that sort of thing." She paled slightly. "In my father's safe I found documentation that I had been adopted. And that my...my birth mother had been a woman who was in the Witness Protection Program right here in Montana."

His attention sharpened, but he kept his face impassive. "I see. Could I have a look at these papers you found?"

She removed a folder from her oversized handbag and handed it to him. "Those are photocopies of everything that seemed relevant. I prefer to keep the originals, as I'm sure you'll understand."

She wasn't as naive as she looked, evidently. He opened the folder, flipping through the documents she'd enclosed.

"You'll see that it was handled through an attorney, and that the birth mother's name wasn't disclosed." She leaned forward, hands straining together in her lap. "But the notes made by the attorney indicate that the mother decided to give up her child because of the dangerous nature of her situation. There's a short note from her asking that I be raised in a good Christian home."

He nodded, scanning quickly, and then looked up at her. "What exactly do you want from us, Ms. Perry?"

She looked startled at the question. "I want to know who my mother was. Isn't that obvious? I need to know what happened to her."

It *was* obvious, unfortunately. She'd just lost the only parents she'd ever known and was probably still struggling to make sense of that loss. Then she'd found this hint of another mother somewhere. Her response was sad but predictable.

"Ms. Perry, I sympathize with you." More than she could know. "But are you sure this is a good idea? Have you talked this over with any family friends, or your attorney, perhaps?"

Her lips firmed. "You think I'm being irrational about this, don't you? Well, I'm not. I have a right to know who my birth mother was."

He glanced down at the papers again. "Maybe your adoptive parents had the right idea in keeping it from you. Information about people who are in Witness Protection is highly classified, and even if it weren't, twenty-two years is a long time."

"I have a right to know." Her eyes pleaded with him. "You can check, can't you? Even if you can't tell me where she is, you could tell her that I'm looking for her? Can't you at least do that much?"

He ought to say no. To shut this off before she just earned herself a lot more hurt.

But he couldn't do that. *Soft,* he told himself. *You're too soft.*

"I'll have a look at the files," he said cautiously. "I can't promise anything. Where can I reach you?"

A smile blossomed on her face. "I'm staying at the Elmhurst Inn." She thrust a card at him. "I've written down the number of the inn and my cell. I'll be waiting for your call."

"I can't promise it's going to be immediate," he said, but he suspected she didn't hear him.

She went out quickly, her step light, apparently confident that he was going to solve her problems.

He doubted it. He glanced at his watch. He had to see Jade, had to find out what, if anything, she might know about her mother's onetime boyfriend. But she was probably at work now, and they'd need privacy for that conversation. He might as well spend a few minutes on a probably fruitless search for Kristin Perry's missing mother.

A half hour later he was reflecting on the fact that he might have been better off if the search had been fruitless. If so, he wouldn't be on the phone to his big brother, wondering what connection an old case of Jackson's might have to Ms. Kristin Perry.

"McGraw here." Jackson's tone was curt.

He resisted the impulse to respond in kind. "This is

Micah. An odd thing has just come up that I thought you should know about."

"So spill."

He took a breath, mentally condensing the story. "A young woman named Kristin Perry showed up here today, looking for information. It seems she's recently discovered that she was adopted and that her birth mother was in Witness Protection here in Montana."

"What did you tell her?"

Was it his imagination, or had his brother's voice sharpened considerably?

"The usual. That we couldn't reveal information about people in the program, that I couldn't confirm anything, that after twenty-two years, it would probably be impossible."

"You did the right thing."

"Yeah. Then I had a look through the files for anyone placed in the program in Montana twenty-two years ago. The only case that fits is one that you worked."

Silence.

He tried again. "I don't think she's going to leave it at that. She's going to keep pushing."

Another silence, for the space of a heartbeat. Then— "I'll be on the next flight out. Call you when I get there." The line clicked. Jackson had hung up.

Well. Obviously his brother remembered the case. Just as obviously it was important, or he wouldn't be dropping everything to hop on a plane to Billings.

There was no point in wondering. Jackson would tell him about it if and when he decided to, and nothing would move him.

Micah mentally calculated the earliest possible time

for his brother to arrive. Not until well into the evening, certainly. He could drive out to talk to Jade and still be back in plenty of time to pick up a few groceries, assuming his brother would want to stay with him.

He rose, reaching for his jacket. Seeing Jade again was business, not pleasure, he reminded himself. And the very fact that he needed reminding told him more than he wanted to know about his feelings.

SIX

Jade unlocked the door to her little house and hesitated. Where had it come from, this reluctance to go into her own home?

That was a silly question. She knew the answer to that. Nothing had been the same for her since the day Micah had walked up to her door.

It wasn't his fault. He was doing his job. She'd always known that Ruby had hovered on the edge of danger for too long. That someday it would come crashing in on her sister, and that Jade could well be caught in the aftershocks.

Pressing aside her reluctance, she stepped inside and closed the door. Since the day she'd moved in, she'd experienced a wave of pleasure each time she walked through the door. Today her only sense was that her house seemed different. Not hers.

She forced herself to go through her usual routine of hanging up her outer clothing, switching from her boots to her fur-lined slippers, putting her keys in the basket on the table. The orderly actions usually comforted her, reminding her that she was in control of her life.

Maybe that sense of control had always been a mirage, with the darkness lurking beyond to shatter it just when she thought she was safe.

She shoved the ugly image away fiercely. She would not let herself think that way. She also wouldn't let herself imagine that someone had been in her home, moving the basket an inch out of alignment, leaving an alien scent on the air. That way lay paranoia. The men who'd killed Ruby were gone, and they'd never bother her again.

As for that mysterious so-called cousin who'd been asking for Ruby in Brownsville—well, there could be some innocent explanation for that, couldn't there? If so, Micah would find it.

Micah. She'd spent the day trying not to think about him, without success. He'd crept into her thoughts while she was meeting with the audio-visual committee, showing the ropes to a new volunteer, even talking to a fellow librarian on the telephone.

She hadn't dreamed up the awareness that had run between them. It had been real.

Maybe that was natural enough. They'd been through an emotional time together, and she'd just wept in his arms. She seemed to hear his murmured words of comfort again, and her cheeks warmed at the memory.

That sense of attraction had been accidental. Micah was probably as eager as she was to forget it.

The phone rang, and she crossed the room quickly to answer it. "Hello?"

"Jade." Her heartbeat accelerated slightly when she heard Micah's deep tones on the line. Maybe he was calling to see how she was after the spectacle she'd made of herself the previous day. Maybe…

"Something has come up that I need to talk with you about." His voice was brisk and businesslike. "Will you be home if I get there in about an hour?"

Apparently she wouldn't have to make an effort to get their relationship back to a neutral level. He'd done it for her.

"Yes, I'll be here." She tried to match his tone. "What is it? Have you found out something about the man who claimed he was my cousin?"

"We'd better wait to talk when I arrive. I'll see you then." He hung up without a goodbye.

Well, the most charitable interpretation was that he questioned the security of her phone line. Feeling oddly unsettled, she wandered to the kitchen, got out an apple and a few crackers, and wondered if she should offer him supper when he arrived.

A glance inside her refrigerator reminded her that she hadn't shopped, but the neighbors had dropped by several times over the past few days, apparently feeling that having one's house invaded by armed thugs warranted the delivery of casseroles.

She was instantly ashamed of the caustic nature of the thought. That offhanded kindness between neighbors was one of the things she loved most about this place. She couldn't allow recent events to turn her bitter.

She got out a chicken-and-rice casserole and pre-heated the oven. Then she took her snack back into the living room to wait for Micah's arrival.

Curling up on the couch, she tried to concentrate on the newspaper, but Micah's face kept intruding. What did he want? Had something new come up? It probably wasn't anything good, or he'd have said something reassuring on the phone.

She tossed the paper aside. News of grain prices and snowmobiles for sale wouldn't distract her for the next hour. She moved instead to the well-filled bookshelves and hesitated for a moment. Her hand hovered over the titles and then she settled on an old favorite.

Snuggled once more on the sofa, she opened and read the familiar first line of *Little Women*.

Christmas won't be Christmas without any presents.

She could almost feel her stress level going down. She would escape into the comfort of a safe fictional world, just as she had at eight or nine. The tale of sisterly love and simple faith would be a good antidote to the horrors of the past few days.

By the time she reached the end of the first scene, the plate had slid from her lap. Frowning, she put it on the floor beside the couch. She must be more tired than she'd thought. She could hardly keep her eyes open, and she never napped during the day.

She pulled the crocheted afghan from the back of the couch, tucking it over her legs. She wanted the story to relax her, not make her comatose. Propping her eyes open, she tried to concentrate on what the sisters would buy Marmee for Christmas.

The book, sliding from her hands, landed on the floor with a soft thud, jerking her awake. She didn't treat books that way. She fumbled, reaching for it, trying to get her eyes open.

But her lids were heavy, so heavy, far too heavy to lift. She'd just drift off to sleep for a bit....

An alarm sounded faintly in her mind, piercing the fog that had invaded her thoughts. Something was wrong. Something was very wrong. She couldn't move, couldn't think—

She forced herself to roll to her side. Her body was even heavier than her eyelids, unresponsive to her commands. She got her legs off the couch, tangling them in the afghan, tried to sit up, and fell forward to the floor, hitting hard.

The jolt roused her enough to send panic surging through her. She had to call for help. The phone was only a few feet away.

She forced her head to lift, trying to focus on the end table. It might as well have been a mile away. She clawed at the carpet, trying to crawl to it. The cord dangled toward the floor, slightly out of reach of her groping fingers.

She lunged forward, her fingers grazing the cord. Fumble. Grasp. Pull. The receiver thudded to the floor next to her.

Reach it, she had to reach it, dial 911—she tried to force her hand to move, but whatever fogged her mind had paralyzed her body. She couldn't do it, she couldn't…

Micah listened to the buzzing that said Jade's line was engaged. Not so surprising, was it? People did talk that long, after all. But he'd been trying to reach her for a good twenty minutes.

The reasoning, rational though it was, didn't dispel the tension the gripped him. Maybe nothing was wrong. But maybe something was very wrong.

He stepped on the accelerator. No other cars on this stretch of road, no one to see or be endangered by the speed at which he moved. His pulse sped along with the vehicle. He was nearly there. If Jade was in danger, if he was too late…

Please, Father, protect her. Be with her. Let me get to her in time.

He turned down the narrow lane to her house, plowing through a few minor drifts the wind had tossed across its surface. He spun up to the house and braked, out almost before the vehicle had come to a stop.

Her car was there. She was fine, surely, but the force that was driving him wouldn't let up. Not until he saw for himself.

He took the steps and the porch in a couple of strides and thudded on the door. Nothing. No sound from within. But she had to be there. The phone was engaged, she'd said she'd be there—

He hurried to the window, cupped his hand to shut out the glare and peered inside. Jade—lying on the floor, still as death.

Drawing back his arm, he smashed his elbow against the glass. The heavy storm window shuddered, but didn't break. It would take something heavier, sharper. He pulled out his gun.

Never draw your sidearm unless you intend to use it. The words from a long-ago instructor echoed in his mind. He'd use it, all right. He smashed the weapon against the window, shattering it.

Shoving broken shards out of his way with his thick gloves, he climbed through.

Gas, so thick it made his head swim in an instant. He had to get her out, quickly, before it felled him, too. He reached Jade, bent to grab her arms, felt himself reel.

No time to check for life, just grab her, drag her across the floor, push her through the window and plunge through himself.

He sucked in a deep breath of cold, clean air and bent over Jade, feeling for a pulse.

It was there, but it was weak, almost undetectable. He had to get help for her. He fumbled with the cell phone, forcing his fogged mind to work as he gave the needed information.

Please, God. Please.

Micah forced himself to concentrate on the utility worker who was checking out the kitchen stove. Checking out the crime scene? It wasn't clear yet that there had been a crime.

His thoughts kept straying to Jade, being tended by EMTs on the front porch. He hadn't left her until he'd seen for himself that she was responding. He wanted to go back out there, find out if she really was all right.

But that wasn't his job. His job was here.

The county sheriff, alerted by the paramedics, had arrived right behind them, eager to get in on whatever was happening. He'd been told as little as possible, but that didn't discourage him.

Now he teetered back and forth from his toes to his heels, unable to keep still for more than a minute at a time.

"Most likely an accident," he volunteered. "You can see for yourself how old the kitchen equipment is. Ole Herb didn't want to put any more money than he had to into this rental."

Micah gave a grunt that could express almost anything. Volunteer firefighters had used their huge fans to vent the house of gas, but it seemed he could still smell it. Maybe that was just what was left in his lungs.

He'd only been exposed to it for a matter of seconds. How long had Jade lain there, breathing it in?

His cell rang. With a muttered apology, he stepped outside to answer it.

"Well?" Arthur Phillips snapped the word. When the chief sounded that irritated, it meant he was worried.

"The paramedics seem to think Ms. Summers is going to be all right. They're still treating her. I haven't had a chance to question her yet."

He'd just had time to hold her and pray while he waited for help to arrive, but his boss didn't need to know that.

"And the cause?"

"The utility workers are still checking it out. It's an old range. It could have been an accident. Or it could have been deliberate."

Some faceless person might have crept into Jade's house while she was at work, rigged a death trap and walked away with no one the wiser. She should never have stayed in this isolated house by herself.

Phillips grunted. "Could have been a suicide attempt, too."

That hadn't occurred to him, and he bit back a quick defense of Jade. Phillips wasn't interested in psychological opinions from his people, just good, solid investigation.

"I'd have expected her to blow out the pilot light and put her head in the oven, then. Not set out a casserole and go into the other room."

Had she planned to offer him a share of that casserole, arriving as he did right at mealtime? If she had, he wasn't sure he'd have had the sense to refuse, and the image of the two of them, sitting at a candlelit table, slid into his mind.

"Maybe. Maybe not." Phillips chased the image away. "Or she might have set up the whole scene to look like an attack. She knew you were coming."

The anger he felt at that comment astounded him. He was careful not to let it show in his voice.

"That would have been a dangerous thing to do. I could have been delayed. She could have died. As it was, she was barely breathing when I got here."

"That's a point." Phillips sounded reluctant to admit it. "Still, she might figure it would convince us she's an innocent victim in this whole mess."

His boss's cynicism didn't surprise him. But Micah hoped he never got that way. He made an indeterminate sound that his boss might take for agreement.

"Try to get her someplace safe until you're able to talk to her. And I understand your brother's coming in— what's that about?"

Micah had to force his mind back to Kristin Perry. Her visit seemed a century ago.

"He gets in sometime tonight. I imagine he plans to brief us tomorrow morning."

Or not. Agencies didn't always share everything they knew with each other.

"Keep me up to speed on that. And on the Summers woman."

"Right." An investigator had to be able to multitask, but he was finding it unusually difficult this time. His own fault, probably, for letting his emotions get in the way.

He shoved his cell phone back in his pocket and returned to the kitchen. It seemed even colder than it had moments earlier. At least that meant it would be impossible for Jade to argue that she could stay here tonight.

The utility worker straightened, making a note on the clipboard he'd dropped on the counter next to the casserole dish.

"So, what do you think?" The county sheriff was too eager to wait on protocol. "Was it an accident?"

The man shrugged, wiping his hands on a rag. "Most likely. Well, you can see for yourself that range is not in good shape."

"Could someone have done it on purpose?" Micah stepped in front of the sheriff.

The workman's eyes lit with interest. He glanced back at the stove, then at Micah. "Sure could. C'mere, I'll show you."

Micah joined him. Together they leaned over to peer at the back of the range. The man reached down to touch a pipe with an oily finger.

"See, there's where the leak is. That joint coulda come loose by itself. Or somebody coulda rigged it. No way of knowing that I can see."

"You didn't find any fresh wrench marks on it?"

"No." He sounded regretful. "But it wouldn't take a wrench to pull it loose. A good twist with your hand would do it."

And leave no marks. He'd have dusted for prints, but he wasn't hopeful. Dissatisfied, he left the sheriff and the utility worker deep in discussion and made his way around the house to the front.

Jade was still sitting on the back of the ambulance,

with her neighbors and the paramedics close at hand. One of the paramedics moved away as he approached, giving him a good look at her. The complete and utter fragility of her face shook him.

"You should be in the hospital." Worry made the words sharper than he intended.

Her face came up, a little spark lighting her eyes. "I don't need a hospital. I'm perfectly fine."

He turned to the paramedic, hoping for some support. "What do you think?"

The woman shrugged. "She doesn't require hospitalization. We can take her in if you want, but they'll just check her out in the emergency room and release her."

"You see?" Jade seemed to take that as a sign the battle was won.

But he wasn't finished fighting. He glanced at the others. "Give us a minute, will you?"

The paramedic shrugged, heading off around the vehicle. The neighbor woman looked ready to argue, but her husband towed her away.

"Fine. If you don't need hospitalization, I'll drive you to Billings and check you into a hotel."

Predictably, she shook her head. "I'm staying right here."

"You are *not* staying right here." He leaned over her, intent on making her understand. "You almost died this afternoon."

"Do you think I don't know that?" A little color came into her cheeks. "I owe you my life. Again."

He shook that off. "If the gas leak was deliberate, it's a criminal matter."

"Deliberate?" Her green eyes darkened with shock. "But my landlord said it was an accident. Ellen was berating poor Herb for not putting a new range in. Are you sure someone tampered with it?"

"There's no proof." He hated admitting that, because it weakened his argument. "But given what's been happening, we can't take any chances."

Jade was already shaking her head. "If there's no proof, I can't see any point in running away from my home. Surely I can stay right here while you investigate."

He counted to ten, forcing down the impulse to snatch her up and remove her bodily, as he'd done when he got her out of the gas-filled house.

"You certainly can't stay here tonight," he pointed out reasonably. "I owe you a new window, for one thing. And for another, the firemen are still venting the house. It's as cold as the inside of a freezer in there."

"All right, all right." She leaned her head on her hand, looking as if that brief spurt of opposition had suddenly worn her out, leaving her exhausted again. "I won't try to stay here tonight. I'll go to Herb and Ellen's."

He didn't like it, but it was probably the best he was going to get, short of taking her into custody. Tempting as the thought was, he really didn't have grounds to do that.

"Promise me you won't attempt to come back here by yourself."

She sighed. "Not until Herb gets a new window put in, in any event. Ellen's not going to give him any peace until then."

She tilted her head back to look at him, and he was struck again by her pallor and the dark circles that lay like bruises on her skin. The longing to protect her swept through him.

"I forgot," she said. "You wanted to talk to me about something. That's why you came."

Yes, he had, but the urgency had been wiped away in the terror of seeing her unconscious.

"It'll keep. I'll come back tomorrow." He touched her then, just a flick of his finger against her cheek as an assurance that she really was alive and well. "Stay safe, will you?"

She managed a smile. "I'll try."

SEVEN

Micah tried to concentrate on the stream of reports that came to his desk the next day, knowing that any one of them might contain the valuable hint that would unravel the confusing case. Unfortunately a certain green-eyed redhead kept intruding on his focus.

He'd already called her once this morning to see how she was. She'd still been at the neighbor's house, but insisted that she felt fine and would be going to work this afternoon.

After a brief, futile argument as to the wisdom of that, he'd given up. She'd probably be safer in a public place like the library, in any event. And however much he might want to hear her voice, he really couldn't justify checking on her again this soon.

If yesterday's incident had been an accident, pure and simple, that was serious enough in itself. If it had been more—

Phillips had cast doubt on that idea in this morning's briefing. Fiddling with a gas connection was hardly the MO of the typical Mafia hit man. Micah had sensed that his boss still leaned toward the theory that Jade had done it herself.

And Micah's only defense—his gut instinct that Jade

was innocent in all this—didn't hold much water without proof to back it up.

And then there was his brother's sudden trip. Jackson's flight had arrived in the middle of the night, so he'd gone to the closest motel instead of staying with Micah. He'd been tight-lipped about Kristin Perry when he arrived at the Federal Building, and was even now closeted alone with her in Phillips's office.

Alone, shutting out not only the rest of the U.S. Marshal Service, but his brother, too. Jackson was the consummate professional, but this secrecy was carrying things too far, in his opinion. After all, the Perry woman had come to him first.

He was still watching the office door when it opened. Kristin Perry emerged first, her bright jacket making a splash of color against the beige background. Then Jackson came out, looming over her, the strong planes of his face giving away absolutely nothing.

"Thank you." She offered her hand, and it was swallowed up in Jackson's.

For a few seconds Jackson stood frozen, clasping her hand, his gaze intent on her face. Micah, watching, could a sense strong emotion being held down fiercely under Jackson's iron control.

And then the moment was over, and Kristin strode quickly down the hall toward the elevator. Jackson watched until the elevator doors closed behind her. Then he turned and walked quickly to Micah.

"What did you think of her?" he asked, his tone abrupt.

Micah leaned back in his chair. It seemed as if he was always looking up at his big brother, both literally and figuratively.

"We didn't talk long yesterday. My impressions? Young, naive, still grieving her parents. Maybe a little too eager to connect with the birth mother whose existence she just discovered."

Jackson's frosty blue eyes were remote. "I'd add a strong core of determination to that list. It won't be easy to discourage her."

Micah refrained from saying that he'd pointed that out in the conversation the previous day. "Is that what we're going to do?"

Jackson surveyed the room. Two criminal investigators worked at their desks, one sifting through the endless series of tips, the other writing a report. Mac Sellers was focused on his computer in the far corner.

"Let's take a walk."

In other words, Jackson had something to say that he didn't want anyone to overhear.

"Right."

Shrugging into heavy jackets, they took the elevator down to the ground floor in silence. In fact, Jackson didn't speak until they were a good block away from the Federal Building.

"You up for hearing a story about the old days?" His brother's question came out on a breath visible on the frosty air.

"Sure thing. How old we talking? Prehistoric?" He matched his brother's long stride.

Jackson's lips twitched slightly. "Not that bad. Twenty-two years ago."

Twenty-two years ago he'd been starting elementary school, and Jackson had been a rookie FBI agent. That simple equation was a measure of the gap between them.

"I take it this is about Kristin Perry."

"In a way." Jackson frowned, eyes seeming focused on the past. "You've probably never run across this, but Sal Martino was actually put away for a time, thanks to the testimony of a young witness."

His mind filled in the gaps in the narrative. "Kristin Perry's mother?"

Jackson nodded. "She wasn't much more than a kid at the time, but already a single mother. She'd had a rough time of it, but she showed a lot of courage, getting on that stand."

"I see." Micah mulled it over, filling in the gaps in Jackson's sparse narrative. "Then she went into Witness Protection."

"She did." Jackson's jaw tightened. "She should have been safe. I assured her that she and her little girl would be safe."

He understood the feeling. At bottom, their job was always to keep the innocent safe. "You said what any of us would." Obviously it hadn't gone by the book.

"I was wrong." Jackson's voice grated. "Somehow they found her. She and the baby were nearly killed in an explosion. They were lucky to survive."

"That's rough." Maybe Jackson had reason to understand his feelings about Ruby's death.

Jackson jerked a nod. "We were going to relocate them again, but I guess Eloise figured she couldn't trust us. She disappeared, leaving the baby behind to keep her safe. She left me a note asking me to be sure that the baby had a good, Christian home and a new life."

Micah blew out a breath, trying to assimilate it all. "So you helped arrange Kristin Perry's adoption. Did you tell her all this?"

"Not all." His wintry expression told Micah how much he was hurting. "How could I? This isn't an ordinary situation with an adopted child trying to find her birth mother. If Eloise is still alive, she has a target on her back. She put Salvatore Martino away, at least until his battalion of smart lawyers got him out again. Sal wouldn't forget that."

"Sal is supposedly dying." He was feeling his way through the situation, weighing the possibilities.

"That doesn't mean the danger is over for her. Even if I knew where she was, which I don't, I couldn't tell the daughter that."

"So you tried to discourage Kristin Perry." Well, it was what he'd done himself, and he hadn't known the whole story.

"*Tried* is the operative word. She's got some of her mother's courage. I told her I'd look into it for her, hoping to buy some time."

"If you found Eloise, if she agreed to go into the program again, she could have her daughter with her, if that's what they both wanted."

"That's a lot of ifs, kid." Jackson halted, turned. "We'd better head back. You've got enough on your plate with the Ruby Maxwell killing. I wanted you to know about this, but I'll deal with it."

Of course he would. Jackson always preferred to deal with things himself. At least he'd trusted him with the background. But...

"You don't suppose there could be any connection between that old case and what's happening now, do you?"

He could see Jackson turning that over in his mind. "On the face of it, I don't see how." His words were slower than his usual incisive tone. "Still, it is odd, Ms. Perry showing up just when you're dealing with a Mafia hit. Maybe a coincidence."

"Maybe." Jade's face appeared in his mind, vulnerable and grieving. "But I don't like coincidences."

Jade parked in front of the library and took her time getting out. Despite her insistence to Ellen, as well as to Micah, that she was fine and she'd be better off going to work, she still felt a bit shaky after yesterday's experience.

But she'd improve once she got busy. Sitting around, listening to Ellen bemoan their failure to put in a new stove hadn't exactly cheered her up. It had been a constant reminder of how close she'd come to death.

She paused to survey the library building as she often did, trying to see it through the eyes of someone who might be persuaded to come in. The turn-of-the-century brick building was one of the oldest in town. Library service had declined slowly over the years, until some determined citizens started putting pressure on the county to hire a qualified librarian and increase the budget.

She smiled with satisfaction as she pushed through the glass-paneled door. Now the library was growing into the kind of vibrant, active place she'd envisioned it could be. Circulation was up, activities had skyrocketed in the past six months, and she had an interested, supportive board behind her.

And will they stay behind you if you keep having odd 'accidents'? The little voice at the back of her mind was persistent.

Yesterday *was* an accident, she told herself firmly. No one could blame her for that. As for the rest of her misfortunes—well, it was up to the marshals to sort that out. She was just an innocent bystander.

She walked quickly through the stacks at the front of the library before going to the circulation desk, just making sure all was as it should be. She had some teenage volunteers who came in after school to reshelve books, but sometimes their grasp of the system was a bit shaky.

The marshals, in the person of Micah McGraw, would handle the aftermath of Ruby's death. He'd already called first thing this morning. She'd steeled herself at the sound of his voice, ready for whatever questions had brought him here yesterday, but he'd just wanted to know how she felt, his deep voice warm with concern.

She couldn't deny that she'd been affected by his caring, to say nothing of the fact that he'd saved her life twice. Still, he'd be forever linked in her mind with what happened to Ruby.

And to him, despite his apparent concern, she was part of a puzzling case, if not a suspect. That was all they could possibly be to each other.

She reached the circulation desk. Allie Brandon, her assistant, greeted her with a worried smile.

"I thought you weren't coming in today, Jade. I don't mind staying on, really I don't."

"I'm better off here." She glanced at the round schoolhouse clock over the desk. "I have story hour at two, and I don't want to miss that."

Allie shook her head, unconvinced. "If you don't mind my saying so, you're looking pretty washed out. I can take over the story hour, or we can cancel it for today. No one will mind. Everyone's heard about what happened to you."

Of course they had. She gritted her teeth, hating the

thought that everyone was talking about her. Wondering about her.

"I appreciate it." She tried for a smile. "Tell you what, why don't we compromise? I'll stay through the story hour, and then if you really wouldn't mind coming in afterward, you can work until closing. Okay?"

Since Allie lived right down the street from the library, it shouldn't be a problem for her to go back and forth.

"Sounds good." Allie's gray-streaked brown ponytail bobbed as she nodded. She pulled her flannel shirt tighter around her. "I'll get my things from the back room and head home. But you call me if you need to leave sooner, all right? It's no problem."

"I will." She wouldn't, actually. She didn't want people thinking she couldn't do her job.

Allie had retrieved her jacket and the oversized bag she always carried and was headed to the door when she stopped. "Good grief, I almost forgot. There was a man here looking for you earlier. I told him I didn't know if you'd be in today."

Her heart gave a funny little flutter. Maybe Micah had gotten away soon after he called.

"That's okay, Allie. I know who it was. He'll probably give me a call."

Allie nodded, waving, and went out, closing the door against the outside chill with a firm hand. Jade followed her to the front and looked out the two big windows, watching as Allie strode off down the sidewalk.

Main Street looked fairly deserted at this hour, with only a few cars parked in front of the café. Not that it was ever all that busy. The children's story hour probably would bring out the most people who'd be on the street all day.

Had Micah hung around White Rock after his visit to the library, or was he on his way back to Billings? Or headed for her house or Ellen and Herb's, looking for her? They should have passed on the road, in that event, but she hadn't seen him. Well, as she'd told Allie, he'd call.

In the meantime, it looked as if she'd have a little quiet to get ready for the influx of parents and preschoolers. Story time had grown from two or three kids once a week to fifteen or more three times a week. She loved the response, but it was a challenge to keep that many children occupied.

She headed for the back room, where she kept the supplies she'd been collecting to use with the children. Someone had donated a monkey puppet in response to a plea she'd put in the paper, as she recalled, that would be perfect to use with one of the stories she planned to read today.

As she organized the books and supplies, the tension that had been riding her began to ebb. She was doing what she was meant to do, and that was the important thing.

What she was meant to do. That was always how she thought of her occupation.

Sister Sally would have said that she was fulfilling the purpose for which God had created her. Jade had always found that a comforting thought—that no matter what chaos disrupted her life, God had a plan for her.

She'd been drifting away from that sureness, and she longed to have it again. Micah had said that when he felt distant from God, it was because he had moved, not God. Maybe he'd been…

Something sounded in the silent library, and her senses jumped to alert. A thud? A footstep?

Probably the front door. The library was open, after all. Gathering up an armload of materials, she walked back through into the main library, prepared to greet whoever had come in.

No one was there. She walked across the width of the main room, peering down each row of shelves, her footsteps echoing emptily on the wide wooden floorboards. Nothing. No one was there.

Moving to the children's section, she put everything down on one of the small tables, frowning a little at her reaction. Or overreaction. She was letting her nerves get the better of her. That had to stop. She was a sensible, rational person. She didn't give way like this.

Now, all she needed was the story rug. She usually rolled it up after each session and stowed it in the back hall cupboard. Glancing at her watch, she saw that she had plenty of time. She adjusted a few of the paper cut-outs on the children's area bulletin board and arranged the books in the order in which she intended to read them. Then she headed back to get the rug.

She was pulling it out of the closet, her arms full, when the noise came again. Nearer this time. Sounding more like a footstep.

Her throat tightened, and the rug slid from her grasp. She forced herself to take a breath. She couldn't huddle back here like a frightened mouse. It was probably someone with a legitimate reason for being here.

"Hello? Is someone there?"

No answer. No answer, but a sound again, like a soft, stealthy footstep. Inside the library, not outside.

"Who's there?" She made her voice sharp, authoritative. Again there was no answer. But something brushed against the wall that separated her from the main section of the library, like a hand, groping along the wall. Close, too close.

Her mind sought for a logical explanation, but some primitive sense overrode it. Run. Get out.

Shoving the folds of the rug out of her way, she bolted toward the back door, fumbled with the lock and tumbled outside into the alley. Slamming the door behind her, she raced along the side of the building, breath coming in cold gasps.

Get to the street. There'd be someone there, someone to help.

Was that the sound of the door behind her? Fear lent wings to her feet. She bolted toward the street, rounded the corner and barreled into a solid male figure, knocking the breath out of her.

EIGHT

Micah grabbed Jade's arms, all of his protective instincts kicking in. He swung her around so that her back was against the wall, his body forming a shield to protect her.

"What's wrong? Are you hurt?" He snapped the questions as he scanned the area, looking for any hint of danger.

"N-no." She gasped the word, shivering.

She'd run outside in fifteen-degree weather without a coat. Something had frightened her badly to make her do that. He tightened his grip, willing her to talk.

"Think, Jade. What happened?"

"I heard someone in the library." She shook her head. Curls tumbled around her face, and she pushed them back with a hand that wasn't steady.

"Someone who shouldn't be there?" The library was open, wasn't it?

"Wait, it was you, wasn't it?" The fear ebbed from her face, replaced by a spark of irritation. "What were you doing, creeping around the building like that?"

"I haven't been inside the library." Obviously she'd heard, or thought she'd heard, someone when she should have been alone.

"But you—"

Ignoring her words, he put his arm around her and marched her to his vehicle, half shoving her into the passenger seat. He reached across to turn the ignition and switch the heater to full blast.

"Lock the door," he ordered, stepping back. "Don't open it until I come back." Before she could argue, he slammed the door and stood frowning at her until she pushed the lock.

He turned to the library, assessing the building quickly. One-story brick, probably an attic and a basement, as well. Too bad he wasn't familiar with the layout. He opened the glass-paneled door and moved cautiously inside, easing his weapon from its holster.

He could call for backup from the locals, but he wasn't eager to involve them if this proved to be nothing, both for Jade's sake and for the department's. There'd been too much buzz about this case already.

Moving methodically, he began to work his way through the building. He was in the main library room, difficult to search because of the alcoves created by the rows of shelves. He moved through, nerves tightening as he rounded each blind corner.

Nothing. He reached the rear without finding a thing out of place, other than a couple of books lying on the floor. He eased open another door, finding what was obviously the library's workroom and break room. One corner was given over to a small fridge and a microwave, with a box of tea sitting on top. The door to the single restroom stood open. Empty.

He reached for the door that must lead to the back hallway, nerves crawling. If anyone was in the building, this was the only place left.

A rug lay half in and half out of a storage closet. There were two other doors, probably one to the attic and one to the cellar, but they were both locked on this side, eliminating them as a place to hide. The back door was unlocked—where Jade had exited, obviously.

He walked back through the building, frowning a little. No one was here now. An intruder couldn't have come out the front. He'd have seen them. But anyone could have followed Jade out the back and quietly walked away.

He stepped outside. Jade slid from his vehicle the moment she saw him. Her face was pale but composed as she came toward him.

"There wasn't anyone inside." She made it a statement, not a question.

"No. An open closet in the back hallway looked disordered."

"That was me," she said quickly. "I was getting the story rug out when I thought I heard someone. Just my imagination working overtime, I guess."

The wind whipped her hair across her face as she looked down the street, probably hoping no one had noticed anything amiss.

"Let's get inside." He guided her in, noting that she hesitated for a fraction of a second before stepping through the doorway.

She rubbed her arms briskly, moving toward the desk. "I'm sorry I panicked. I guess I'm still more upset than I thought from yesterday. This old building makes noises all the time, especially when it's windy."

"Which it always is this time of the year."

If Jade wanted to dismiss it, he had no evidence to

support any other explanation. Just like yesterday and the gas leak.

"Yes. That must be it." Her face flushed with embarrassment, as if she thought making a fuss without justification was a crime. "My assistant told me you'd come by earlier. I'm sorry I wasn't here."

He blinked. "I wasn't here earlier. What made her think it was me?"

"She didn't. I mean, she said a man had come by, asking for me, and I just assumed it was you because you'd said you were coming today."

He rubbed the back of his neck, trying to assess the situation as if he looked at it cold, without knowing Jade or the circumstances of Ruby's death. "Did she describe the man?"

"I didn't ask." She raised her hands, palms up. "I'm sure it's nothing. It could have been anyone. I've been advertising for new volunteers, so maybe it was someone wanting to talk about that."

He'd reserve an opinion for the moment. "Can we go someplace where we can talk? Maybe the café?"

She was shaking her head before he'd finished. "I can't."

"I guess we'll have to talk here, then." He'd rather get her away from the site of her scare. And she could probably use some hot coffee or soup after being outside.

"I can't do that, either." She glanced at the round schoolhouse clock mounted over the desk. "I have story hour starting at two, and a bunch of preschoolers will be swarming in here any minute now."

"Can't someone else do it?"

Her lips tightened. "I don't want anyone else to do it. I can't afford to have people saying I'm not doing my job.

They're probably talking enough already." She waved him toward the door. "Go, get some coffee. Come back at three, and we'll talk then."

He didn't like it, but a mother with a couple of kids in tow came in, looking at him curiously, so he went.

Jade sorted through the books she'd picked out, mentally rehearsing her presentation. It should be a comforting act, but the peace she'd felt earlier eluded her. Maybe that was gone for good. Maybe her life would never return to what she thought was normal.

No. She wouldn't let that happen. If she lived in fear, even if the bad guys never harmed her, they'd have won.

The sound of the door opening set her nerves jumping, but she rose and smiled, welcoming a tide of small children and parents as they flowed into the room. The children's chatter quickly set the library echoing happily, and a colorful mountain of jackets, hats and mittens rose on one of the tables.

The distraction was working. She felt herself relaxing, heard her responses to the children become more and more natural. Once they were gathered on the story rug, with parents browsing through the stacks or seated on the small chairs behind the children, she'd regained her usual composure.

She launched into the first story. The lively, dramatic form that she could never have used with adults came naturally when she told stories to children.

This was her element. This was where she belonged, seeing their eyes widen and their small faces light up as they responded to the magic of story.

By the time the hour neared its end, she was back to

her usual self, but far more exhausted than telling a few stories would account for. Apparently passing out from gas had taken more out of her than she'd been willing to admit.

She turned a page in the final book. Once this was over, she'd be glad to accept Allie's offer to relieve her for the rest of the day.

The front door opened, letting in a drift of cold air before it shut again. She sent a quick glance that direction. It was a man, bundled up to his eyes against the cold. Probably a father, come to pick up his child.

She finished the tale of Curious George's adventures, the children clapping when the little monkey triumphed as always.

"That's all for today, boys and girls. Thank you for being such a great audience. Don't forget to check out some books for Mom and Dad to read to you at home, okay?"

They surrounded her, eager to comment on the story or share something new that had happened at home. The man who'd entered late came toward them. She expected him to pluck a child from the group, but instead he stared at her.

Her heart sank. He wasn't going to mention her problems in front of the kids, was he?

"Eloise!" He barked the name, startling her.

"I'm sorry?" She made it a question. Surely he wouldn't call a small child with that tone.

"You are Eloise, aren't you?" He moved closer, nearly stepping on one of the children who'd sat down to pull on boots. His hazel eyes were as cold as ice, as if he didn't even notice. "I saw you react."

"My name is Jade. I don't know any Eloise." Except the one in the children's books, and he didn't look like anyone who read children's stories.

Apprehension shivered down her spine. She pushed children toward their parents. *Get the children out of here*, her mind screamed. *Nothing must happen to them.*

"That's right," he said, smiling thinly. "Get the kiddies out of the way. Then you and I will go someplace quiet and have a little talk."

She took an instinctive step back, putting her palms out as if to fend him off. Like a snake striking, he grabbed her arm.

Please, Lord. She took a breath, trying to think. The children—that was what was important now.

"Mary Louise, will you take the children out the back door, please?" She made her voice clear and calm as she spoke to the mother she knew best. She met the man's eyes. "I'll talk to you. Just let them go."

Mary Louise hesitated for just a moment, her face white as she took in the situation. Then she began shepherding mothers and children toward the back door.

Finally they were out. She could breathe again.

"Let's go, Eloise." His grip tightened painfully on her arm, compelling her to move with him toward the front of the library.

"My name is not Eloise," she repeated. "Who is she? What do you want with her?"

He ignored her protest. "You have a debt to pay." He shoved her toward the door.

She banged into it, making her head swim. The man caught the release bar and shoved it open. She stumbled as he propelled her out into the cold.

"That's right," he said. "No fuss. We don't want anyone else getting hurt, do we? We'll just go for a drive so we can talk in private."

He steered her toward the alley. His car must be there—she could hear the motor running.

Advice from a long-ago self-defense class echoed in her mind. *Never get in a car with an assailant. Scream, kick, bite, do anything you can, but don't get in the car, or you'll be at his mercy.*

"No!" She screamed the word at the top of her lungs, swinging her free arm at him. "Help!"

He struck her, hard, cutting off the cry, making her head spin. He grabbed both arms before she could react, nearly lifting her off her feet. He'd carry her to the car, she couldn't get away—

She struggled, kicked, tried to scream again, but he got his hand over her mouth, the leather of his glove cutting off her breath. No one would hear, by the time the women got help, it would be too late—

A shout from down the street, the sound of pounding feet, sending a fresh burst of adrenaline through her. She fought, kicked, struggled—anything to make it harder for him, to give help time to reach them.

He let go with one hand, reaching toward his pocket, maybe for a gun, but the footsteps were closer now, and the voice that rang out was Micah's.

"U.S. Marshals. Let her go. Put your hands where I can see them."

Cursing, the man threw her toward the building. She hit hard, dropping to the ground, bracing herself for a shot.

It didn't come. She caught a blurred impression of the man disappearing around the corner, heard the slam of a door and the roar of a powerful motor.

Then Micah was there, lifting her gently, his hands

strong on her arms, his breath fast. "Stay here." He propped her against the wall and ran around the corner, his gun out.

He'd be too late, she thought with what was left of her mind. The man had too much of a head start.

Micah was back in a moment, his arm circling her, supporting her. "Easy," he said. "Take it easy."

She took a breath, trying not to give way in front of him. And said the thing she'd never wanted to stay.

"You were right. I can't stay here. It's too dangerous for other people." She sucked in another breath on a sob she couldn't stop. "I'll have to go away."

When they reached Jade's house, Micah left her in the truck while he did a quick check. It was unlikely the attacker had come here, since any vehicle would be clearly visible from the lane, but the man had already staged an attempt in front of a library full of kids. No use depending on him to act rationally.

The house was empty and looked undisturbed. He returned to his vehicle to lead her inside. She looked numb. As if she was past feeling anything. She hadn't spoken a word since those moments in front of the library.

"Don't worry," he said, more to fill the silence than because he thought the words would actually do any good. "I'm checking you into a secure hotel in Billings. You'll be safe there."

She shook her head but not in negation, more as if to shake off his words. "It doesn't matter."

Her voice had lost its music. She sounded defeated. He'd been too relieved that she was actually letting him get her to a safe place to react to the pain she must be feeling.

He didn't know what to say. He watched as she dropped her jacket on the sofa. She looked around the room as if she'd never been there before.

"I'm sorry." He was, not that it did any good. "I don't want to rush you, but if you just throw some things in a bag—"

She nodded, walking toward the stairs. "It won't take long."

"Take as much time as you need."

Protocol said to get her under wraps as quickly as possible, but his instinct overrode that. He couldn't hurry her, not now. She was too fragile at this point.

She moved slowly up the stairs, holding on to the railing like an old woman. Once she disappeared, he let out the breath he'd been holding. Pulling out his phone, he called Phillips.

"Are you on the road yet?" Phillips asked abruptly.

"We're at her house. She's packing what she needs. No sign that anyone's been in here."

"They're probably long gone. It's too bad you couldn't get a description of the vehicle. At least we could have set up roadblocks."

He gritted his teeth. There was no answer to that. If he'd been a few steps quicker, he might have a description. All his attention had been on Jade. When he'd seen her go down, his heart had stopped.

Apparently taking his silence for agreement, Phillips went on. "Get her here as soon as possible. Your brother is waiting to sit in on the questioning."

"Right."

He let himself think about the woman named Eloise

and the story Jackson had told him. Eloise. What on earth did she have to do with the attacks on Ruby and Jade? Given the emotion Micah had sensed in him, he'd just bet Jackson wasn't going to be leaving anytime soon.

"Call when you're on the road." Phillips cut the connection abruptly.

Micah pocketed his cell and paced across the room. The window had been repaired. Obviously Herb Trask had been on the job.

Someone had put the curio shelf back up on the wall, though there were no crystal bells on it. All in all, the room looked as if the turmoil of the past few days had never happened. It was as neat and orderly as it had been the morning he'd stepped inside to tell Jade her sister was dead.

And changed her life in the process.

No, not him. He couldn't blame himself for that. The shooters would have come after her anyway, for a reason none of them understood.

Still, he got that he was connected in her mind, probably irrevocably, with the chaos that had taken over her life. She'd probably never stop seeing him that way.

Chaos. That was the word Ruby had used to describe the twins' early lives with their mother. Jade had gotten away from that, through a process more difficult than he could imagine. And now it had descended upon her again.

He could picture her as a young girl, taking refuge in the library where she could read stories about happy middle-class families, doing all the things he'd taken for granted. And then she'd gone home to find her mother drunk and no food in the house. Or worse.

Jade's footsteps sounded on the stairs. She came down

slowly, carrying a small suitcase and a laptop bag. He met her and took the bags from her.

"Is there anything else you need?" His gaze swept the room. "Anything else that will make you more comfortable in a hotel room?"

Some of the life came back into her eyes. "I'll take some books."

"I can pick up something new and bring them to you," he offered, counting the seconds until they were on the road toward Billings.

She bent over her bookshelves. "I'd rather have some old friends." She ran her fingers along the volumes tenderly, as if they really were friends. She didn't hurry. Looked at one, put it back, pulled out another.

He shifted his weight from one foot to the other. Phillips would be irate that this was taking so long. And he ought to be preparing Jade for the questioning she'd face once he got her to Billings.

But he had the strongest sense that this process was important, even crucial, to her. Books had been her refuge in childhood. She was turning to them again now, in this time of crisis, seeking the security and order that were missing in her real life.

He forced himself to stand still. To wait patiently. And reflected that seeing the particular books she chose might tell him a lot about her, if he could get a look at the titles.

Finally, holding four books in the crook of her arm, she walked back to him.

"Would you like me to take those?"

She shook her head, seeming to retire again into that blankness that must be a protection for her.

"Nothing else you want to take?"

She crossed to the sofa and picked up the afghan that lay across its back, folding it and adding it to the stack with the books. She stood, looking around the room, and her gaze seemed to linger on the empty shelf against the far wall.

"I'm sorry about your bell collection. They must have meant a lot to you."

He meant it as an opening, but she just shook her head. Whatever it was about the bells that had made her weep, she wasn't going to share it with him.

She slipped on her jacket, zipped it and picked up the books and afghan, along with her bag. "I'm ready." Her tone was expressionless.

When they reached the door, she stopped, staring back at the room.

"Will I ever be able to come back to this life?" She tilted her head back to look at him, and her green eyes were glazed with tears.

The sight cut him to the heart. He wanted to reassure her, but he had no reassurance to give that would be honest.

"I don't know. I hope so."

She nodded and marched out the door.

NINE

The numbness was starting to wear off. Jade pressed her fingers to her forehead, staring out the vehicle's window as they rolled past miles of snow-covered countryside. Each mile took her farther from everything that was dear to her and closer to a murky future.

"Are you all right?" Micah's voice was warm with concern. "I know this has to be hard for you."

"Hard? Giving up everything I love about my life? Yes, you could say that."

She was instantly ashamed that she was taking it out on him, although there was no change in Micah's expression. He still wore that neutral cop's mask that didn't give away anything of the man behind it.

She shook her head. "Sorry. I know it's not your fault."

"I'm here." He sent her a sidelong smile. "You need to take it out on someone."

She couldn't return the smile. She could only stare at her clasped hands.

"Why?" The word burst from her. "Why? I don't understand why this is happening to me. I'm not guilty of anything."

I'm the innocent one in the family. That was what she

wanted to say, but she couldn't. Maybe she hadn't broken any laws, but even so, could she claim to be guiltless?

"You mean, why does God let good people be hurt?" Micah's strong hands tightened on the steering wheel. "I guess that bothers me, too. I see too much of it in my work."

"What do you do about it?" She studied his sharply chiseled profile. "How do you make sense of it?"

"I'm not sure I always do." This time his smile was wry. The cop mask was off, at least for the moment. "I'm not some kind of super-Christian, Jade. I just know that we live in a fallen world where bad things happen. But one thing I'm sure of—God can bring good out of even the bad things that happen to us."

She let that filter through her mind. "It's hard to see anything good coming out of Ruby's death."

"I didn't say it would happen immediately."

"Or ever?" She challenged him, suddenly wanting to dent that assurance of his.

"Ever is a long time. See how you feel once things are back to normal."

"Right now it's hard to imagine my life will ever be normal." Fresh pain knifed through her.

"I don't want to promise what I can't deliver, but I believe we're going to solve this." He hesitated. "I think I understand what your home means to you. I have a place like that, too."

"Really?" That surprised her, somehow. "I thought men weren't as attached to their homes as women."

"Don't you believe that." He nodded toward a house and barn that sat on the left side of the road, sheltered by pines. "That place reminds me of mine. You drive back a lane a half mile or so, and you come to my little holding—a small house, barn, shed, a few acres. It's not much, but it's mine."

If she'd thought about it at all, she'd have pictured him living in a rented, furnished condo in Billings.

"How do you keep up with a place like that? It seems to me you're always working."

"I don't do it as well as I'd like to," he admitted. "My neighbor's a retired cop, living his dream of running a few cattle. He helps out with my animals."

"Animals, too." This was a side of Micah she hadn't imagined. Lawman, Christian, rancher—what else?

"More than I should have, I guess. Two horses, a dog, a couple of goats, a dozen steers. Jesse, that's my neighbor, wanted to give me some piglets, but I drew the line at that."

"Even so, it sounds like quite a menagerie. You must be fond of animals to take on that many."

"Guilty. In fact, I once planned on becoming a veterinarian." He paused for a heartbeat. "I changed my plans when my father was killed."

She'd wondered if his father's death had anything to do with his career. Here was the answer.

"Do you ever regret the decision?"

He pondered that for a moment. "I don't think I regret it. Sometimes—well, I see people like my brother, who seem to have been born for the job. Makes me think I'm missing something. But regret? No. I like being one of the good guys."

He was that. Despite her occasional anger at him and the resentment that sprang up without warning, she didn't doubt who he was at heart. One of the good guys.

She'd like to say that, but somehow she couldn't. It would be too personal, and they shouldn't venture into that territory.

The buildings of Billings were visible on the horizon, a reminder that this ride would soon be over. It had been a comforting respite from all the ugliness that had invaded her life, but now she had to face it.

She nodded toward the city on the horizon. "What will happen when we get there?" She tried not to sound apprehensive, but she suspected she didn't fool Micah.

"You'll need to talk to the investigators who are working the case." He paused. "My half brother, Jackson McGraw, wants to talk with you, as well. He's a Special Agent with the FBI in Chicago, specializing in organized crime."

Micah had a brother in the FBI. She digested that. "Why Chicago? I mean, why is he interested in what's happening here?"

"It may tie in with a case he's working on." Micah didn't sound evasive, precisely, but clearly he wouldn't be as open about anything professional as he had been about his spiritual life.

"I still don't see how I can help. I don't know anything. I can't begin to imagine why those people are after me."

"Sometimes the most inconsequential thing can be important." He stared at the road, not at her, as traffic thickened. "For instance, there's the thing I'd wanted to talk with you about, before this latest attack."

She'd nearly forgotten. That worry had been swallowed up in larger ones. "Just say it, whatever it is."

"A name popped out at me when I was looking through some old background records on Ruby. Do you remember a man named Georgie Messina?"

"I don't think...you mean, Uncle Georgie?" The name came back to her from more years than she could immediately count. "He was a friend of our mother's, not Ruby's?"

"'Uncle' Georgie?" His tone put the word in quotes. "He must have been pretty close if you called him that."

"Not really. All of Mom's boyfriends were 'uncles,' at least until she fell out with them." The words left a bad taste in her mouth.

"Georgie Messina wasn't anyone special, then?"

She hugged her jacket around herself. Funny, this need she had for comfort whenever she had to talk about the old days. "He was good to Ruby and me. Not like some of them. He'd always bring a couple of pizzas when he came over, and he always remembered what we liked on them. Why? What could that have to do with Ruby's death? We couldn't have been more than eleven or twelve at the time."

"Uncle Georgie ran numbers for the Mob."

She wasn't sure how to respond to that. "I didn't know. I wouldn't have. Ruby might. She was more streetwise than I was. But even so, it was years ago."

"Like I said, some things seem to have meaning and don't. Some are coincidental or completely irrelevant, but we have to weed through them to get to the truth."

"So that's the kind of thing they'll want to ask me." A shiver snaked down her spine as she thought about the upcoming interview.

"Could be. Just don't be alarmed if they want to go over things again and again."

In other words, she was in for a grilling. It was kind of him to try to prepare her. But then, that kindness was one of the things she recognized in him, in spite of the barrier his profession put between them.

She studied Micah as he negotiated the increasing traffic going into the city. Strange, how close she'd come to this strong, dedicated man in such a short time. Before she met him, she'd lived a cautious life, wary of others, unwilling to trust.

Her relationship with Micah had happened very quickly. It would end just as fast.

The interview with Jade had been going on too long. Her pallor and the circles under her eyes alarmed Micah. True, no one had been openly antagonistic, but they'd taken her through her story so many times, asking questions from a slightly different angle, that it would be an ordeal for anyone.

She'd been through a lot in the past few days. His hands grasped the edge of the conference table. In a moment he'd have to interfere....

His gaze met that of his brother. He didn't think he gave anything away, but Jackson seemed to probe his face and come to a conclusion.

"I think we've done as much as we can today." Jackson's level voice cut short a question from Micah's boss. "Ms. Summers is probably more than ready for a break."

Arthur Phillips looked annoyed for an instant, but then his expression smoothed over. "Of course. We appreciate your willingness to help, Ms. Summers."

Jade didn't even attempt to smile. That was probably beyond her at the moment. "I can't see that I've been much help."

"We never know what information will pay off in the long run." Jackson gave her the catch-all answer. "Deputy Marshal McGraw will take you to your hotel and see that you're settled, if you wouldn't mind waiting for a few minutes for him." His tone made it clear that she didn't really have an option.

"Fine," she murmured. She didn't slump in her seat, but he'd guess it took an effort to keep her spine straight.

"Maybe we can get you some coffee while you wait?" Jackson glanced at Phillips, who in turn looked at Mac Sellers, who'd been making notes.

Mac started to rise.

"No, thank you anyway." She frowned at the foam cup on the table. "I've had enough coffee. I'll just wait."

"Very good." Jackson collected the rest of them with his gaze, and they left the interview room.

"Guess you want me to start transcribing this." At a nod from Phillips, Mac headed for his desk with his notes and the recorder.

"Let's go over our impressions while they're fresh in our minds." Jackson led the way into Phillips's office and raised his eyebrows at the older man. "Your thoughts?"

"On the face of it, there's no way to connect Jade Summers with the Mob at all." Phillips sounded as if he resented that fact. "So why are they after her? As for the gunman calling her by the name of a woman who once testified against the Martino family—" He shook his head, glaring at Micah. "Are you sure that happened?"

"It was overheard by a half dozen witnesses." He kept his voice calm, knowing that Phillips's irritation was caused by the frustration they all felt.

"And that's another thing." Phillips drove a hand through his thinning hair. "What kind of Mafia hit man kidnaps a victim in a library in front of witnesses? This sounds more like amateur hour."

"It's certainly not the usual MO," Jackson said smoothly, intercepting any reply from Micah. "I've told you about the old case. If Vincent Martino is after the woman who put his father away, which would fit with what my informant says about him wanting to pay tribute to his dying father, why would they attack Ruby? I suppose you could argue that Ruby led them to Jade, but how could Ruby be connected? The only thing is…"

He let the sentence fade, unusual for him.

Micah's attention sharpened on his brother's face. "What is it? Do you see a connection?"

"Not a connection, exactly. But I noticed Jade's eyes. Green. I suppose Ruby had the same. Eloise had green eyes."

Phillips gave a grunt of frustration. "Vincent Martino may not be the most sensible of men, but even he can't think to avenge his father by killing all the green-eyed women in Montana. And why would he think Eloise is here at all? You said she dropped out of sight after the attack that injured her baby. She could be anywhere."

"True. It would make a lot more sense for Martino to put a bounty on the only active witness we have against him." Jackson's glance flickered to Micah. "You know about that?"

"I've been briefed on Olivia Jensen," Micah said. "We've got her safely tucked away until Vincent's trial comes up in the spring. But I agree—you'd think he'd be going after her."

"If we didn't know that those first two shooters were Mafia, I'd think this whole thing was a figment of somebody's imagination." Phillips tossed a file on his desk. "And then there's that phony cousin who turned up in Brownsville asking questions about Ruby after her death."

"You get anything more on him?" Jackson rested a hip on the edge of the desk.

"As much of an ID as we're likely to get. We had the locals talk to the woman, show her a few pictures of Mob mug shots. Lo and behold, she picks out Sonny Guardino, a minor soldier with the Pittsburgh Mob who apparently aspires to be a hit man. But he arrives late for the party."

Jackson's brow knotted. "Maybe show it to Jade Summers, as well. I suppose it's possible that their lines of communication aren't the best, but it's odd."

"Odd like everything else about this case. We've got lots of speculation, but not much in the way of facts." Phillips frowned at Jackson. "Where do we go from here? The way I see it, both the old case and the active one are more in your bailiwick than ours."

"First off, we'd better think about increasing security on the Jensen woman." Jackson's face tightened. "I'm not going to risk losing the only witness we have against Vincent Martino. Meanwhile…"

"Jade Summers has to be protected." Annoyed that Jackson seemed to be putting someone else first, Micah tried not to glare at his brother. "She's become a target, whether it makes sense or not. She's lost her sister and her whole life has been disrupted."

Jackson's brows lifted slightly, probably in surprise at Micah's passion.

He'd have to be more careful. He shouldn't be feeling anything for Jade, but if he did, he certainly shouldn't let anyone know.

"Protecting her is the idea," Jackson said. "We keep her out of the line of fire until we figure out what's going on. Every contact I have in Chicago is being tapped for info on what Vincent Martino is up to. I've got a team working full-time on that end."

"So we'll keep following up every line of inquiry here," Phillips said. "That's all we can do. Good, old-fashioned detective work will solve this in the end."

"Go." Looking at Micah, Jackson jerked his head toward the door. "Take Ms. Summers to her hotel and make sure she has everything she needs. Right now, it looks as if what she could use most is some reassurance." His mouth twitched slightly. "You'll be a lot better at that than I am."

Phillips nodded. "Agent McGraw is right. Get her settled. We'll go at all this with fresh minds tomorrow. There has to be a loose end somewhere. Mafia or not, nobody's that good at keeping secrets. Somebody knows what's going on, and why. We'll get there."

They would. Micah didn't doubt that. He just prayed it wouldn't be too late for Jade to get her life back again.

"You have to eat something." Micah looked remarkably stubborn on the subject as they approached the door of the hotel room assigned to her.

"I'm too tired to eat." It was an effort to keep putting one foot in front of the other. "I just want to get some sleep."

If she could. If her slumber wasn't haunted by visions of Ruby lying dead, or the frightened faces of the mothers and children at the library.

Or middle of the night fears for her future. What if the county library didn't want her back after all this upheaval? What if the federal agents insisted that she, like Ruby, had to disappear into Witness Protection? What if they never came to a resolution, and she was left to spend her life wondering if she was safe?

She rubbed her forehead, trying to erase the thoughts, as Micah inserted the key card in the slot. Apparently she didn't have to wait until 3:00 a.m. for her mind to climb onto that dreary treadmill.

Micah moved her gently to the side of the door and put down her cases. "Stay there until I've checked the room."

"I thought this place was supposed to be safe."

"Double-checking never hurts." He stood to the side as he pushed the door open, and then he reached inside to flip the light switch.

She'd thought she couldn't feel anything, but her stomach churned as he moved inside. If someone was there, if Micah was hurt because of her…

Nothing happened. He moved into the room, and she heard the muffled sounds he made as he checked closets, the bathroom, probably even under the bed. Finally he returned and guided her in.

To her surprise, it was more than just the standard room she'd expected. They'd gotten her a two-room suite, with a small living room that actually looked welcoming. The lights of the city shone beyond the large window until Micah pulled the drapes. Then he carried her suitcase through into the bedroom.

Glancing through the door after him, she looked longingly at the queen-size bed, but she couldn't collapse yet. Not until Micah was gone.

"Thank you." She managed a smile as he returned to the living room. "I'll be fine now."

He crossed to the desk, depositing her laptop there, and picked up the telephone. "I'm calling room service. What do you want?"

"Nothing. I told you…" She let that die off at the stubborn expression on his face. She sighed. "Fine. Soup, preferably chicken if they have it. An order of toast. A pot of decaf tea."

His dark lashes swept down over what was probably a look of triumph in his eyes. He pushed a button and relayed her requests to room service. Hanging up, he turned back to her.

"I don't want to sound like a worried mother, but promise me you'll try to eat something."

"I don't recall my mother ever worrying about what I ate, but I appreciate the thought. I'll try. Really. You ought to get some rest yourself. This day feels as if it's been a hundred hours long already."

"Just a few precautions I need to share with you first."

"Don't open the door without knowing who's on the other side? I have stayed in hotels before." She'd sit down on the floral-patterned sofa, but if she did, she might never get up.

The corners of his firm mouth lifted. "It's always a good rule. Look, this place is as safe as it's possible to be without putting a twenty-four-hour guard on you. No one followed us here, I promise."

"I trust you, Micah." The words surprised her. She didn't trust easily, and she hadn't even known she was thinking that.

He looked almost shaken at that. "I'm glad. It wouldn't be surprising if you blamed us for the chaos we've brought into your life."

"Maybe I have been. Blaming you, that is. Things certainly haven't been the same since the morning you knocked on my door." Her voice quavered a little as she remembered the news he'd brought.

"I'm sorry." He took a step closer, touching her arm gently. "I know how hard this has been on you. I wish we had some answers to give you, instead of just endless questions."

"Your brother is very good at that. I couldn't tell whether he believed a word I was saying." She should resent that feeling, but it was all a part of this bizarre world in which she found herself.

"That's the FBI training. He affects me that way, too. I'm never sure what he's thinking."

She blinked at that. "But he's your brother." She'd always been almost too aware of Ruby's thoughts. Sometimes she'd wished she could shut off that understanding.

"It's the age difference."

"Still, you rely on him." Maybe she was really asking if Jackson could be trusted with her safety. Her future.

His hand moved reassuringly on her arm, warming her skin even through the knit of her sweater. "I know he's a person of great integrity, just like our dad was. I only hope I can live up to that."

The hint of self-doubt touched her heart. "I don't think you need to wonder about that." She looked up at him, seeing nothing but warmth and caring in the chocolate-brown depths of his eyes. "Even when you've been driving me crazy, I haven't questioned your honesty or your devotion to doing your best."

His eyes seemed to darken. "Thank you." His deep voice grew husky. "That means a lot to me. I…"

The sentence faded away as his gaze explored her face. Her breath caught in her throat. It was as if he looked into her heart and saw all the safeguards she put upon it. They seemed to crumble at his touch.

"Jade," he whispered her name, and the air seemed to reverberate with the sound. "I shouldn't…"

His lips found hers, tentatively at first, and then surer, claiming her as if this had been destined to happen from the moment they met. She put her hands on his arms, thinking she should push him away. Instead she drew him closer, reveling in the gentleness of his kiss, the strong protection of his touch.

Micah had stood by her during the worst moments of her life. He knew all the bad things and cared anyway. He'd saved her life more than once. She didn't have to guard herself with him.

He drew back at last, letting his fingers trail down her face as if reluctant for the moment to end. "I shouldn't have done that. I've just broken all the rules. If my brother knew…"

"I won't tell." Her voice sounded ridiculously husky.

"I should go." He let go of her suddenly, and she felt cold where his hands had been. "You understand, don't you? Until this is over, I can't treat you as anything other than a witness."

"I understand." She tried to put assurance into the words. "It's all right."

He seemed to take comfort from that. "I'll call you in the morning." He crossed quickly to the door. Paused. "Put the dead bolt and the chain on. I won't leave until I hear you do that."

The door swung shut behind him. She snapped the dead bolt, flipped the chain into place and laid her hand on the door, imagining him on the other side of it. She didn't move until she heard his footsteps receding down the hall.

She was falling for him. She shouldn't. There was no future in it that she could even imagine, but that didn't seem to matter.

TEN

Every force that drove Micah was centered on Jade—protecting her, comforting her, caring for her. That's what he should be doing. Instead he was driving a couple of hours away from her to meet with another woman.

Not just another woman. Another witness. Jackson and Phillips had agreed that someone should meet personally with Olivia Jensen to alert her to the need for increased security. Since he's already been briefed on the woman because she might be connected to Ruby's case, they'd decided he should go.

Maybe they thought he was getting too close to Jade. If they thought that, they'd be right.

He'd taken a giant step over the line last night. He ought to be beating himself up with regret over it. But he wasn't. Usually his instincts and his training worked in tandem. Not this time.

He was nearing the small town café where the meet had been arranged. For the past fifty miles he'd been tempted to pick up the cell phone and call Jade, just for the pleasure of hearing her voice. If he was going to call her before this meeting, it had to be now.

He glanced at his watch. Too early. As exhausted as

she'd been, he hoped she'd taken advantage of the chance to sleep in. He'd wait, no matter how much he wanted to hear her voice.

He parked a half block down from the café, sitting in the car for a few minutes. No one had followed him—he was sure of that. And nothing looked out of place on the quiet block.

He got out, zipping his jacket. Nobody sauntered down the street on a day this cold. That would be suspicious in itself. Instead he strode quickly to the café.

A bell tinkled when he opened the door. He stepped into a warm atmosphere scented with freshly brewed coffee and something that must be cinnamon rolls.

The plump, gray-haired woman behind the counter waved. "Have a seat. I'll be right with you."

Obviously the morning rush was over. The only occupants were two elderly men sitting in the corner with coffee mugs in front of them, looking as if they'd been there for a decade or so.

And Olivia Jensen, sitting in a booth on the opposite side of the room. He walked over, arranging his face in a friendly smile. As far as anyone else was concerned, they were acquaintances, meeting for a casual cup of coffee.

"Hi. It's nice to see you." He said it loud enough to be overheard as he slid into the booth opposite her. "Ms. Jarrod, I'm Deputy Marshal Micah McGraw." He lowered his voice on the introduction and showed her his ID, cupping his hand around it in case the elderly residents were more interested than they appeared.

She stared at him, looking anything but relaxed and casual, her wide blue eyes strained and worried. "What's wrong?" The words were a tense whisper. "The message

I got just said to meet you here. Why didn't they tell me what's wrong?"

Sometimes secrecy could be carried too far. Whoever had relayed the message could have spared a sentence or two of reassurance to the woman.

He smiled, patting her hands, clenched tightly together on the red-and-white-checked tablecloth. "We're two old friends, getting together for coffee, remember? There's nothing wrong."

That wasn't quite the truth, but they didn't know that the problem was related to Olivia, and there was no sense in alarming her if he could help it.

She managed a smile, some of the tension fading from her face. Some, not all.

Before he could say more, the woman who seemed to be waitress, cook and probably dishwasher, too, hustled over to their table, pulling a pad from her apron pocket.

"Cold enough out there for you folks?"

"Hey, it's a balmy twenty degrees out there," Micah replied. "Practically a heat wave for January."

She chuckled. "You got that right. What can I get you?"

He glanced across the table. "What will you have?"

"Just decaf tea and toast for me, please. Whole wheat, if you have it."

Her pallor reminded him of Jade, and the order for tea and toast did, too. Was that a universal female remedy for stress?

"You got it. And you?" She waited, pen poised over the pad.

"Coffee," he said promptly. "Are those cinnamon rolls I smell?"

"You bet. I just took a pan out of the oven."

"One of those, then."

She bustled away again, swinging by the other table to refill cups and exchange a little friendly banter.

"I'm sorry." Olivia's smile turned more genuine. "I'm afraid I'm not very good at this."

"No worries," he said easily, although truth be told, he had plenty. "How are you getting along? Blending in all right? Getting used to the weather?"

"I suppose so. It's not really that much worse than a Chicago winter."

Remembering the wind off the lake, he nodded. "Nothing's happened recently that's made you uneasy or alarmed you?"

"No." Now she did look alarmed. "Why? There is something wrong, isn't there? Just tell me."

Like Jade, she didn't want beating around the bush when it came to bad news. He was the one who recoiled from blurting it out.

"As far as we can tell, it's nothing to do with you, but there has been an increase in Mob activity in the state. Again, there's no indication it's aimed at you. Just the opposite, in fact."

Jackson had been very clear about what and what not, to tell the woman.

"What kind of Mob presence?" She was keeping her anxiety under control, though it couldn't be easy.

"I'm sorry, but I can't discuss the specifics with you." He really was sorry, but she probably didn't believe that.

Her jaw tightened, and she crossed her arms, as if to shield herself. "Are you moving me to a new location? Is that it?"

"There doesn't seem any reason to do that. The FBI is contacting the county sheriff's office and asking for increased surveillance. They'll be on the alert, and you can call them at any time, day or night. Otherwise, you shouldn't notice any disruption in your normal life."

Her mouth twisted, as if in pain. "It's a little late for that, don't you think?"

"Yes. I'm sorry." His voice roughened. He thought of Jade and the losses she'd endured, of Ruby, dying too young. "You've paid a high price for being in the wrong place at the wrong time. I wish I could say it was going to get easier, but I don't know that."

She sucked in a breath, as if to steady herself. "Thank you." There was a reflection of tears in the blue eyes. "You're the first law enforcement person who's really seemed to understand what this is like."

He didn't know what to say. If he understood, it was because of his relationship with Jade—a relationship that shouldn't exist.

The waitress arrived then with their order, and they talked about the weather until she'd gone.

Micah looked at the plate-sized cinnamon roll she'd put in front of him. "Sure you won't have some of this? It's a lot bigger than I anticipated."

"No, thanks." She nibbled at the edge of a piece of toast. "You people will let me know if there's any new information, won't you?"

There was an edge to her voice that troubled him. Was she having second thoughts about cooperating? Or was something else wrong?

"We will, of course. I'm sure it seems as if we've forgotten you, but someone is constantly working the case."

She nodded in acceptance, but her gaze was distant. Distracted.

"Is something else worrying you, Olivia?" He leaned forward, intent on her face. "If so, I hope you'll tell me. If I can help—"

"You can't help with this." The words came out with a passion that startled him. She put one hand on her midsection in a protective gesture that spoke volumes. "I've just recently realized that I'm pregnant."

"I see." He took his time reacting, trying to gauge her feelings. "Is there anything you need? Have you found a doctor?"

"That side of it is all right. I just…" She shook her head in a pained movement. "This makes me feel so much more vulnerable. I have another life to protect now."

"I see that." He put his hand over hers in a gesture of support. "It means we have another life to protect, too. We'll take that seriously, I promise."

"Thank you." The tension in her face eased. "I'm glad I told you."

He was, too, but it sent his thoughts back to the story Jackson had told of the young woman who'd given up her baby rather than risk its life.

That old case, brought back to life when Kristin Perry walked into his office, couldn't have anything to do with Olivia.

He just prayed the same devastation didn't await her.

Jade hadn't been in the hotel for even twenty-four hours, and already she felt as if she were ready to crawl out of her skin from the inactivity. How did anyone live in such limbo, unable to make plans, unable even to have routine human contact?

How had Ruby done it? She'd never really appreciated what Ruby had gone through during that time of waiting to testify, waiting to be resettled. Ruby had been far more impatient than she was, far more used to excitement in her life. How had she managed?

Maybe, for Ruby, it had been a respite. Her life, always on the edge, had tumbled over into danger. Maybe she'd welcomed the enforced idleness. Certainly, from what Micah had said, Ruby had found peace in her new life, even if it hadn't been the life of her choosing.

She paced across the small living room, stopping to stare at the phone. Micah hadn't called yet. She'd expected to hear from him.

She pressed her hands to her cheeks, feeling the heat in them. That was a cliché, wasn't it? Waiting for a man to call again after that first kiss?

She hadn't expected it. At least, she didn't think she had. And yet, when it happened, it was as if every moment since she'd met him had arrowed straight toward that one.

She touched her lips lightly, imagining she could still feel his kiss. It was crazy, in the midst of all this turmoil, to be acting like a teenager with a crush.

She could call him. She reached toward the phone, imagining his voice warm in her ear. He'd given her his cell number and said to call if anything worried her.

Probably that anything hadn't been meant to include her schoolgirl reactions to his embrace or her need to hear his voice. The feelings were too new, too untested. And far too much weighed in the balance against them.

She'd turn the television on and get caught up on what was happening in the world. There'd be plenty of crises in the world that made hers seem very small.

Ten minutes later the phone rang. She sprang at it, snatching it up.

"Hello?" Her voice was ridiculously breathless.

"Is everything all right with you? Any problems there?" Micah's voice, just as warm as she'd hoped, sounded in her ear.

"No problems at all, unless you count boredom." She sank into the desk chair, cradling the receiver with both hands. "If I ever wanted to be less busy, I've changed my mind."

"Sorry about that. I'm afraid it can't be helped at the moment." A bout of static interrupted his voice. He must be on his cell.

"Where are you?"

Why aren't you here? That was what she wanted to say, but she stifled the words.

"I can't tell you that." He sounded distant, as if she'd broken some unwritten rule by asking the question. "Sorry."

"I see. I mean, I understand. Will I see you soon?" That was a reasonable question to ask, surely.

"I don't know. I'm on my way to the office right now." Again that distant note, and now she knew what was happening. He was trying to reestablish the boundaries between them, boundaries they'd both crossed the previous night.

She understood. Really, she did. But somehow that didn't prevent a ripple of anger from running through her.

"I'll talk with you later, then." She kept her voice level with an effort. "Goodbye."

She didn't wait to hear him say goodbye. It might sound too final. She hung up.

The room wasn't really big enough to walk off her bad temper. Instead she opened her laptop and booted up. Micah had told her not to let anyone know where she was. He hadn't said she couldn't be in touch with people. She could at least check her e-mail.

A few minutes later she realized her mistake. She had e-mails, plenty of them. Friends, acquaintances, library board members, all wanting to know what had happened at the library yesterday, none of them accepting the official clampdown on information.

Who had that man been? Why had he come to the library after her? What was going on?

She couldn't answer any of the questions. And if she didn't have an explanation, people would imagine the worst.

How long would her job last, given this blow? If she were on the library board, she wouldn't want to employ someone whose presence brought danger into the children's story time.

She sucked in a breath, thinking of the children's faces during those terrible moments. Then she opened an e-mail to the library board.

Slowly, choosing every word with care, she began to write, skirting carefully around the full truth. Apparently someone believed she'd witnessed a crime, putting her in danger. The U.S. Marshal's office had taken her to a safe place until they could arrest the criminal. She was sorry, and she hoped they could manage without her for a brief period of time.

She paused, fingers on the keys. Should she offer to resign? Maybe she could cling to a tiny fragment of hope for a little longer. Without adding anything else, she hit Send.

She shut the mail program and sat for a moment, head resting on her hands. *Please.* The word came from somewhere deep inside. *Please.*

Slowly she opened the desk drawer, knowing what she'd find there, and pulled out the Gideon Bible.

For a long moment she just held it in her hands, remembering. Sister Sally had given a Gideon Bible to each of them when they were in fourth grade. Hers lay in the drawer of the nightstand at home.

What had happened to Ruby's? Discarded long ago, or kept, so that Ruby had it to turn to when life had brought her back to God? The study Bible she'd brought from Ruby's apartment had been relatively new, although well used, with notes written in the margins.

The thought took her by the throat. She should have packed the books she'd brought from Ruby's, instead of leaving them on the bedside table at home. She might have found comfort in them now.

Pastor Davison's people had probably cleared Ruby's apartment by now. He'd see that her things went to people who needed them. She should call him and thank him again for all his kindness. In the rush and sorrow of Ruby's funeral, she hadn't said enough to him.

But she couldn't even call him now, not without checking with Micah first. He said he didn't want any former connection with Ruby's life. Tears stung her eyes. She was cut off, isolated from everyone and everything familiar, until this was settled.

A tear splashed on the dark red cover of the Bible. She

wiped it away with her fingers, hesitated a moment, and opened the scriptures.

In times of trouble, turn to the Psalms. Sister Sally's voice echoed in her memory. *You'll find the strength you need there.*

Strength, she'd said. Sister Sally had never been one to offer easy comfort. Strength to face the burdens of the day—that was what she'd asked, for herself and for the children she brought to Jesus.

Jade began to read, turning from one familiar Psalm to another, feeling the words sink deep within her. Touching the painful places, bringing healing. Dropping onto her fears, bringing strength.

Finally she turned to the much loved words that had been read at Ruby's funeral.

The Lord is my Shepherd, I shall not want...

A sob ripped through her. She sank from the chair to her knees, turning back to her Heavenly Father and feeling His arms welcome her.

Micah knew something was wrong the instant he walked into the office. The atmosphere of tension was palpable, showing itself in averted gazes and rapt attention to computer screens or reports.

Mac jerked a nod at him. "You're wanted upstairs. Right now."

"What's going on?" A summons to the office of the U.S. Marshal in charge of the region didn't come along every day of the week.

Mac shrugged, looking annoyed that he didn't have an answer. "Just get up there."

He turned on his heel and headed for the elevator, stomach churning. This had to be something bad. Jade? His heart skipped a beat. But he'd spoken with her not half an hour ago. If something had happened to her, he'd have been contacted via radio or cell.

When the elevator doors opened, the secretary at the nearest desk nodded toward the door to the conference room. He was expected, apparently.

Those who were seated around the polished table looked up as he entered, wearing similar expressions of gravity...the chief, Jackson, Arthur Phillips and two other criminal investigators who'd been working the Ruby Maxwell case.

He focused on Phillips, his immediate boss. "You wanted to see me?"

"We've had another killing." Phillips's tone was harsh.

Micah's heart stopped. Jade...

"A woman named Carlie Donald." He shuffled through the files in front of him and pulled one out. "It went down last night. Harper took it." He gave a crisp nod to one of the investigators.

Dave Harper probably hadn't had any sleep, and his usually wry, amused face held a serious expression. "The locals didn't call as quick as they should have. Apparently thought it was a domestic gone bad. She and the boyfriend had gone at it before. He'd been out drinking, came home to find her dead. Strangled."

Micah slid into a chair, pushing thoughts of Jade to the back of his mind. "Carlie Donald." He repeated the name. "I'm not familiar with her. Any Mafia connection?"

Someone must think so, or else why was Jackson sitting in on this meeting?

"She testified against a small-time Mafia soldier," Jackson said. "She went into Witness Protection, but didn't change her lifestyle, apparently."

"Liked to live on the edge," Dave said. He handed a sheaf of photos to Micah. "Could be she picked up a guy and it turned violent. Or could be the boyfriend, if he got home earlier than they think."

"A coincidence," Jackson said the word as if it were a curse. "That's hard to take."

"Everything isn't connected to the Mob," Phillips snapped. "If you think…"

Micah stopped flipping through the photos, staring at one. "That mark on her palm. What is it?" He was vaguely aware of having interrupted his boss.

"Graphite, according to the lab." Dave consulted a report. "Lot of places she could pick up something like that. It doesn't necessarily relate to the murder."

He flattened the photo on the table. "I'm afraid it does." He looked, not at his boss, but at his brother. "Ruby had the same black mark on her palm."

Jackson's breath hissed. "The black hand. The Mafia."

Phillips held out his hand for the photo, and Micah gave it to him. He studied it for a long moment. Then he looked at Jackson. "I owe you an apology, Agent McGraw."

"So this is Mafia-related." The chief marshal spoke for the first time. Former military, he didn't get rattled easily, and he didn't show alarm now. "This is your area, Agent McGraw. What are they doing? Do these killings relate to the Bureau's case against Vincent Martino?"

"Could be." Jackson's mouth clamped on the words. "More to the point right now, how did the Mob find two unrelated female federal witnesses who have both been relocated to Montana?"

Silence, for a long moment. Micah's gaze went from face to face as each person in the room assimilated the unpalatable truth.

"So." Arthur Phillips's face tightened to a rigid mask and said what they were all thinking. "There's a leak. Here. In this office."

ELEVEN

"Effective immediately, the investigation into the deaths of Ruby Maxwell and Carlie Donald, and the attacks on Jade Summers, will be turned over to FBI Special Agent Jackson McGraw."

The chief marshal stood as he spoke, an intimidating figure at the end of the conference table. Silence greeted his words. He spun on his heel and walked out of the room, looking as if he barely managed to refrain from slamming the door behind him.

Everyone in the room knew how he felt. It was how they all felt. Someone in their office, one of the very people they trusted to watch their backs, was in the pay of the Mob. That deed dirtied every single one of them.

Even worse, how could they look at each other without wondering if the person they were looking at was the one?

Micah read the question in the averted gazes and the mumbled responses of the others as they filed out of the room. They'd been shamed by the realization, then shamed again that the investigation had been taken out of their hands.

Finally Micah was alone with his brother. A wave of

indignation rose in him. "I'd trust any of those people with my life."

Jackson stared at him for a moment, expressionless. "Would you trust them with Jade's life?"

That question punched him right in the gut. "I...I don't know."

Jackson's face was hard. "Then you should understand why your chief had to do what he did."

He understood. But somehow that didn't seem to make the humiliation any better. He murmured a quick, silent prayer for guidance.

"Okay." He took a breath, steadying himself. "I get it. One person in this office is a traitor, so everyone is suspect. You think I don't understand how serious that is? Jade's location at the hotel could already be compromised. You have to—"

Jackson held up a hand, shutting him off. "I can't discuss the case with you, Micah."

He opened his lips to argue. Shut them again. Jackson wouldn't bend. Everyone who knew him understood that about Jackson.

For a long moment they stared at each other, while a chasm grew between them. There was nothing left to say.

Micah walked out of the conference room. He got on the elevator, trying to focus. One thought kept blanking everything else out. His brother didn't trust him.

No, that wasn't fair. Jackson trusted him as a person. He knew that. But Jackson didn't trust his judgment in this case, or his ability to act impartially.

He should go straight to his office and find out what Phillips wanted him to do. He had no choice but to walk away from the case that now belonged to the FBI.

Jade was in danger. The traitor could be giving away her location right now.

Jackson would act to safeguard her, but would it be soon enough? He would have to wait for his own team to arrive, hamstrung by the fact that there was no one here he could trust. And in the meantime, who was keeping Jade safe?

The elevator doors opened on his floor. He glanced in at the desks, listened to the dispirited silence. Then he punched the button to take himself down to the parking garage.

He couldn't take the chance. If he did nothing else, he'd move Jade to a different hotel and then let only Jackson know where she was. There would be repercussions, but he couldn't help that now.

Acting on instinct, he thought wryly. His big brother would have a few sharp words to say about that.

Minutes later he was in his vehicle and covering the few blocks to the hotel, eyes flickering to his mirrors to be sure no one followed him. He yanked out his cell phone and punched in the hotel number, then Jade's room number. He should give her a heads up that he was coming, tell her to get packed and ready to move. Every wasted minute meant that the killers could be getting closer.

The phone rang. And rang. And rang. His tension ratcheted up with each unanswered ring.

Where was she? She should be there. She'd been told not to leave the room without an escort. He let it ring until the line switched over to the hotel's answering system. Frustrated, he ended the call, not wanting to leave a message that someone else might hear.

Where are you, Jade? Where are you? His fingers tightened on the steering wheel. She could be in the shower, unable to hear the phone. That must be it. She wouldn't leave. At least—

Could Jackson have already moved her? Possible, but if so, wouldn't he at least have told Micah that she was safe?

Probably not. Jackson followed the rules, and right now the rules said that Micah was shut out of the case.

But his instincts were riding him, just as they had when he'd rushed to find Jade unconscious from the gas leak. Telling him that Jackson wouldn't have had time or manpower to move her. Telling him that she was in danger.

Please, Father. His mind fumbled for the prayer. *Wherever Jade is, be with her now. Surround her with Your protection. And get me there quickly.*

Around one more corner, cutting it short, and then he was driving down the ramp into the underground parking garage. He headed for the back, where the elevator was. A few more minutes, and he'd…

Jade. The sight jolted him like a physical blow. Jade, alone, stepping off the elevator. Alone. What on earth was she doing?

She paused for a moment, glancing around the gray, echoing interior of the garage, and then started walking to her right, where a rank of parked cars sat.

He accelerated toward her, touching the horn to draw her attention. She spun, that banner of red hair swinging out, vivid against the forest-green jacket she wore.

She saw him. Recognized him. And then she whirled and ran in the opposite direction.

Panic ripped through Jade like an earthquake, tearing apart pieces of her heart. It was Micah. She could trust Micah, couldn't she?

Trust no one. That was what the FBI agent had said when he called. Trust no one. Not Micah. Not anyone who said they'd come from the marshal's office.

Her running feet took her along the rows of cars on the right side of the garage. The agent had said Jackson McGraw would be there. He'd said he'd be waiting. Where was he?

Micah was coming. She could hear his vehicle, bearing down on her. Her instincts urged her to turn and run toward him, but the fear was too strong. It propelled her feet, stumbling now as she scanned the ranks of cars.

A maroon sedan pulled out of a parking space toward the end of the row, turning against the lane markers to accelerate toward her. It must be Jackson—

Then she saw. A hand, a gun, extended from the window of the car. Pointed toward her.

She veered, hearing a muffled report that echoed from the concrete walls of the garage. No time to think. Just run, dodge behind the nearest car, find shelter.

She crouched behind a car, heart thumping loudly in her ears. Safe for a moment, but they'd pull up parallel to her and have a direct shot. She couldn't stay here, but where could she go?

She heard the roar of a motor, the screech of tires— too late, too late to evade—

Micah—it was Micah, leaping from his vehicle. He reached her in a heartbeat, grabbed her by the arms. She felt his strength as he lifted her, practically carried her over the few feet to his truck. He threw her into the vehicle, shoved her to the floor and slammed the door.

In an instant he'd slid behind the steering wheel, stamping on the accelerator without even closing his door. She was thrown against the dash as the vehicle veered, making a U-turn. Metal shrieked—they must have hit one of the pillars. The door slammed shut even as something pinged against it.

A bullet, her numbed mind acknowledged. The person in the other car was shooting at them.

Tires screamed. Micah rounded the turns, heading for the exit. There'd be a bar across the lane; he'd have to stop. The pursuers would be on them before he'd identified himself—

A crash, and the vehicle shuddered but kept going. Pieces of the barrier flew in all directions. She thought she heard someone yell.

They surged up the ramp to the street, taking the turn into traffic on two wheels as horns blared and brakes shrieked.

Bracing herself against the seat, she looked up, focusing on Micah's face—stern, unyielding, intent.

He'd saved her, yet again. She could trust him.

Trust no one. But she had to.

He didn't shift his eyes from the street ahead, but she sensed his attention on her.

"Get into the seat. Buckle up. I need you to watch for them."

She hesitated, fear riding her.

"Do it," he snapped.

Choking down the fear, she slid into the seat, fastening her seat belt. "I'm in."

"Where are they?"

She turned, scanning the crowded street behind them. *Trust no one.* But she had to trust someone, and the other men had guns. Besides, this was Micah.

"I see them. They're a half block back, maybe more. In the far right lane."

Jerking a curt nod, Micah tightened his grip on the wheel. They were nearing an intersection, the light turned yellow—

Without slowing, Micah took a hard left through the intersection, ignoring the horns that blared in their wake. He sped along the wide street.

She struggled to orient herself. She had only been to Billings a handful of times since moving to Montana, and the city layout was still a mystery to her. They were somewhere in the downtown business district, that was all she could be sure of.

"Are they still there?"

She turned in the seat again, craning her neck. "I don't see them. Maybe we lost them."

"Not that easily."

He took another turn. Then another. Did he have a destination in mind, or was he just trying to lose the pursuers?

"Where are we going?"

His brow furrowed, but he didn't answer.

"Micah, where are you taking me?"

"Someplace safe." He snapped the words. "Keep watching for them."

She obeyed, trying to force herself to think rationally. *Trust no one.* That message had been from Micah's own brother. Hadn't it? Maybe that had been a trick.

But Micah had saved her. Her thoughts spun in futile circles.

She wanted to trust Micah. But why wasn't he calling for help? Why wasn't he heading straight to the Federal Building and safety? Surely that was the most sensible thing to do. The small worm of suspicion gnawed at her, refusing to be ignored.

He switched off the busy road onto a side street lined with smaller shops.

"Still no sign of that car." She watched the street unroll behind them. "We must be safe."

A grunt was his only answer. Obviously he didn't trust her judgment. Well, what was new about that?

Her handbag lay on the floor, where it had fallen when Micah pitched her into the vehicle. Her cell phone was inside. If she tried to take it out, to call someone, what would Micah do?

A park ran along the right side of the street, deserted at the moment except for a dog-walker or two. Micah veered suddenly, pulling into a road that ran through the park, slowing down.

He took one turn, then another. She could only hope he knew where he was. Then, when a grove of trees screened them from the street, he pulled to the curb and stopped.

Her breath caught. What—

He turned, his hand shooting out to grasp her arm. "What's going on? Why were you out of your room?"

"I didn't..." She stopped. Started again. "I had a phone call."

"A call." Frustration edged his voice. "What call was important enough to make you leave the hotel room without letting me know? Who called?"

She forced herself to meet his gaze. "Your brother. The call was a message from your brother."

His face tightened, and she wasn't sure how to read his expression. "My brother. What did he say?"

"I didn't talk to him." She'd have known Jackson's voice, she thought. "It was a different FBI agent, with a message from him."

"And what was the message?" He sounded as if his patience was strained to the breaking point.

She closed her eyes briefly, remembering the voice on the phone. "He said he was calling for Special Agent Jackson McGraw. He said there had been a security leak from the marshal's office, and Special Agent McGraw was coming to meet me." She hesitated, knowing the rest of it would hurt him. "He said not to trust anyone, especially not anyone from the marshal's office."

Micah didn't actually wince, but the fine lines around his mouth and his eyes deepened. "You figured that meant don't trust me. And you ran."

"What did you expect me to do?" Anger came to her rescue. "Ignore his instructions?"

"Instead you nearly got yourself killed." He slapped the palm of his hand against the steering wheel.

Killed. Her stomach lurched. She hadn't had time to process that yet.

"Was it true, what he said?" Her fingers linked together. She needed something to hold on to.

Micah stared out at a picnic pavilion covered with snow. He didn't meet her eyes, and that in itself told her it was true.

"Another woman in Witness Protection in Montana has been killed." His jaw tightened, a muscle twitching in it. "Somehow the Mob knew how to find her, just as they seemed to know how to find Ruby. The only place we can see that information coming from is our office."

She sucked in a breath, trying to comprehend it. "Is that how those men knew where to find me today?"

"Probably."

"But your brother said…"

He glared at her, his brown eyes as hard as that chiseled chin. "Get this through your head. That so-called message was a trap. The call didn't come from the FBI. Jackson would never ask you to leave the safety of your room to meet him."

The word chilled her, and a shiver slid down her spine. "So someone in your office told them where I was. I never was safe there. They'll find me, no matter where I am."

"No." He barked the word, his fingers closing over her wrist. They slid under her jacket sleeve, warm against the skin. "Don't tell yourself that. They're not omnipotent. Now that we know there's a leak, we'll find it. We'll keep you safe."

She wanted to believe that. Wanted to believe him.

Be careful, the nagging little voice whispered at the back of her mind. *He didn't call for backup. He hasn't called in to report what happened.*

"Shouldn't we go back to the Federal Building?" She didn't look at him when she asked the question. She didn't want him to read the doubts in her eyes.

"It's not safe. We don't know who the leak is. Until we do, we can't trust anyone there."

"But…" It was insane. The very people who were supposed to protect her couldn't be trusted. "What about your brother? You can call him, can't you?"

He frowned. "I will, but not until I've taken you someplace safe."

Again the doubts came. Her instincts said to trust him, but she wasn't a person who acted on instinct. She was logical, rational, a person of method and order, her life organized like the card catalog of her library.

As if he sensed her thoughts, his fingers moved on her wrist, weakening her will. "Jade, I'm trying to do what's best for you. You can't be anyplace that can be guessed by the traitor. Jackson has sent for his people, but until they get here, we're on our own."

"Is that what he said?" She seized on his words. "Does the FBI know what you're doing?"

He didn't answer. Instead he let go of her wrist. She put her hand over the place where his had been, trying to hold on to the warmth she felt when he touched her.

Micah shifted gears and pulled onto the street again. "There's a guy I know—he was actually the first person I placed in Witness Protection. Stan Guthrie, his name is. He runs a lodge up in the mountains. It's not on the list of safe houses, so even someone with access to that couldn't know about him."

"You want to take me there." It sounded logical enough, the way he'd put it. Still, the doubt wasn't easily dispelled.

"It's the safest place I can think of. Stan won't ask questions, and he owes me. He'll keep you safe until we know who's selling us out to the Mob." His voice chilled on the words.

"You're sure it's someone in your office." If he was telling the truth, that had to be a hard situation for him, having to admit that someone he worked with was betraying him. Betraying all of them.

"The location of witnesses is tightly guarded. We've always said that the U.S. Marshals have never lost anyone in Witness Protection who followed the rules. If this is the first lapse in security—well, it better also be the last."

He flipped open his cell phone. "I'll call Stan and make sure he's there. Then we'll head out of Billings. Okay?"

Did she have a choice? She nodded, wanting to believe him. Wanting to trust him.

But still unable to completely silence her doubts.

TWELVE

Micah didn't breathe easily until they were well away from Billings, headed west on I-90. He still couldn't relax, but at least he'd gotten Jade safely away. If their pursuers hadn't caught up to them by now, they must have lost them.

Jade hadn't said a word in miles. He shot a sideways glance at her. She huddled in the seat, her arms wrapped around herself as if for comfort.

His heart clenched. She needed a bit of comfort. After everything else that had happened to her, finding out that someone from the agency she counted on to protect her was in league with the bad guys had to be a harsh blow.

How many more strikes could she take? Ruby had been hardened—tough, streetwise, ready to adapt to whatever life swung at her. Jade wasn't any of those things. Funny, that twins who'd been raised the same could turn out so very different.

His stomach growled, reminding him that it was well past lunch time. His mind flickered back to that breakfast he'd shared with Olivia, before his professional world fell apart. It might as well have happened months ago.

He'd have to find a place to eat. If you let yourself get too hungry or too tired when you were on the job, the chances went up that you'd make a mistake. They were coming up on an exit, with a truck stop that was probably as good as any.

"What say we stop and get some lunch? Is that okay with you?"

His voice sounded too hearty, even to himself, maybe because he was so aware of letting her down. His agency, his office, someone he worked with had betrayed them, and he hadn't seen that coming.

Jade roused at his question. "That sounds good." She glanced out the window. "I guess I am getting hungry."

She sounded detached. Too detached. He could only pray she wasn't giving in to hopelessness.

He wouldn't let them get her, no matter what it cost. But there was no point in telling her that again. Only deeds would convince her now, not words.

"Maybe we ought to order something to go. We still have a long drive to the mountains."

And longer still until he'd safely stowed her away and told Jackson what he'd done. And listened to the flak he'd take for his unilateral action. Were they already wondering why he hadn't gone back to the office?

No, they wouldn't wonder. They'd know. By now they were aware that a vehicle whose description fit his had crashed through a barricade at the hotel's parking garage. They'd know Jade was gone. With any luck, they'd have an APB out on the maroon sedan.

He switched his cell phone on to check. Plenty of calls, most of them from his brother or his boss. He was going to be in plenty deep trouble by the time he finally got in touch with them. How many years of desk duty was this going to earn him?

He hesitated a moment and then switched the phone off again. No point in listening to the irate calls telling him to bring Jade back at once. Not when he had no intention of doing that. He'd call when she was safe, not before.

He pulled into the truck stop, automatically scanning the area, alert for any sign of the maroon sedan or anything else that looked suspicious.

It was on the late side for lunch, so there wasn't that much traffic at the truck stop. A small group of truckers clustered in front of their rigs, seeming deep in conversation, their breaths forming a little cloud around them.

An older couple exited the restaurant and climbed into their RV as he watched. Florida plates. What on earth were they doing in Montana in midwinter?

"Looks okay." He cut the engine. "Let's go in."

Jade nodded. She opened the door and slid out while he was still reaching for the door handle. He climbed out, stretching a little, and turned toward her.

Jade took off running across the lot, headed for the group of truckers, screaming.

Shock immobilized him for a moment. Then he raced after her, nerves standing on end from that scream.

"Jade! What's wrong?" He was about ten feet away when she reached the men—close enough to hear what she said to them.

"Help, please, help me! That man—he's abducting me!" She swung, pointing an accusing finger directly at him.

Anger battled hurt...anger that she'd drawn attention to them this way. Hurt that after everything that had happened between them, she so clearly didn't trust him.

"Jade, come on." He took a few steps closer. "This isn't going to help."

One of the truckers moved in front of her. Big, burly, well over two hundred pounds of muscle, probably. The others followed his lead, forming a wall between him and Jade.

He sent them a warning glance. "Look, guys, you don't want to get involved in this. Just step away and let me handle it."

They didn't budge. The wiry guy on the end reached into the cab of the nearest rig. He pulled out a baseball bat and smacked it suggestively against his palm.

The big guy held up a fist the size of a ham. "You're the one who better step away, bud. And do it fast, before we decide to take a piece out of you."

Baseball Bat wasn't waiting. He took a stride toward Micah, swinging the bat. "I say we take him out first. Then call the county mounties and let them deal with what's left."

Micah balanced on the balls of his feet. He had no wish to be on the receiving end of that bat. And no choices left. He pulled out his badge.

"U.S. Marshal," he snapped. "That woman is in my custody."

Baseball Bat blanched, but he still had some bluster in him. "She says different."

"You've seen my ID. Either you get out of the way or I run you in for interfering with a federal officer. That what you want?"

For an instant it hung in the balance. Then, as if someone had given a signal, the men melted away like snow on a summer day.

Still, it would be safer just to get going. They'd eat later.

Micah advanced on Jade and grabbed her wrist. She pulled back. He tightened his grip.

"Enough, Jade. Don't make me handcuff you."

Her gaze flew to his. "You wouldn't."

"Try me."

That was anger speaking, but it seemed to do the trick. She walked along docilely enough to the vehicle and slid into the seat when he held the door open. She stared straight ahead, refusing to look at him, but color flamed in her cheeks.

So she was mad. He was, too. Anger was the safest resort at this point, because if he let go of the anger, he'd know exactly how much it hurt.

Jade wrapped her arms around herself, holding on tight. If she didn't, she just might fly into a million separate pieces, and what good would that do?

She stole a glance at Micah. He stared straight ahead at the highway, his face as cold and hard as the macadam. If he really was the man she hoped he was, she'd hurt him badly. Doubt was a cold, hard ball in the pit of her stomach.

When that man had advanced on him with the baseball bat, she'd been flooded with the urge to retract it all. To say anything that would protect him.

He hadn't needed her protection. All he'd had to do was pull out that badge. It was like a magic talisman in a fairy tale, allowing him to do whatever he wanted. Good, in the right hands. In the wrong—

"What possessed you?" He shot the question at her, not taking his eyes from the road. "Don't you realize how dangerous that stunt could have been?"

No answer came to mind, except the simple truth. "I wanted to be safe."

A tiny muscle pulsed in his jaw, the only sign of movement in his taut expression. "Keeping you safe is my job. I thought you trusted me."

"Trust works both ways, Micah." The spurt of anger warmed her.

Now he did look at her. "What do you mean? I trust you."

"Trust me?" Her voice went up without volition. "How can you say you trust me? You haven't explained what's going on. Why are you taking off on your own? Why haven't you been in touch with your brother? You aren't doing any of the things it would be logical to do, and yet you expect me just to go along with you."

"Jade…" His expression changed. Softened, as the neutral, expressionless, cop mask he'd been wearing slipped away. "I'm sorry. Look, I tried to explain the situation to you."

"Not very well." Maybe he had attempted some sort of explanation, but it hadn't been enough.

He blew out a breath. "Look, we don't know who the leak is, only that he or she has access to way too much confidential information on the Witness Protection Program. It can't be clerical staff or maintenance, because they don't have access to that. This can only be someone with a security clearance as high as mine."

"Another deputy marshal." She was thinking, not reacting, and that was good. She was at her best when she followed her intelligence, not her instincts.

"Or a criminal investigator. Those are the only possibilities that I can see. So I can't follow any of the normal procedures, because if I do, he'll be able to guess what I'm up to. Where you are."

She considered that, logic still battling her instinctive urge to trust him. "You make it sound as if he's omnipotent."

"Not that. It's one person, not the whole department. But until we know who that one person is, no important information can go through there." His brown eyes grew darker with what seemed to be caring. "Important information like where you are."

That was sensible enough, but… "What about your brother? You know you can trust him. You haven't called him."

His lips twisted a little, as if in pain. "Jackson is in charge of the investigation now. When I tried to talk to him about the need to move you, he cut me off. Dead. As if I was nobody to him."

He probably didn't realize how much pain threaded through his words, and how much it revealed of the person he was. Her heart twisted.

"I'm sorry," she said softly. "I know how much that hurt."

"Jackson goes by the rules. Everyone who knows him knows that. Ordinarily—well, I wouldn't like it. But I'd go along with it. Not this time."

His words seemed to vibrate in the enclosed space. "Why not this time?" she almost whispered.

"Because I let my fear for you get in the way."

He said it quietly, but it shook her as nothing else could.

"I'm sorry." Her voice thickened. "I don't want to cause problems for you with your brother."

He blew out a breath that might almost be a sigh. "Don't think that. This is between Jackson and me, and it's not really anything new. He's always thought of me as a kid."

"How do you think of him?" She probably already knew the answer to that.

He shrugged. "My big brother the FBI super-agent?

He's a hero, like our dad. Someone I've tried all my life to live up to. And never quite made it."

She thought of what he'd said and what he hadn't said. "He loves you."

"I don't doubt he loves me." That betraying muscle twitched in his jaw again. "But respect me as a federal officer? That's another question."

She finished the thought. Because of this, he might never earn his brother's respect. Despite Micah's protestations, it seemed very likely that she'd caused a breach between them.

"He's been trying to reach you, hasn't he?"

Micah's strong hands tightened on the wheel. "My brother, my boss...you name it, they've all been calling me."

In other words, he was getting himself into serious trouble trying to protect her.

"Micah, why don't you just call him? Tell him what you're doing and why. Surely he'll understand that you're just trying to keep me safe. He knows you. He won't doubt you, even if he doesn't agree."

"If I call him now, he'll tell me to turn around and bring you back. We'll be right where we were." His forehead creased in a frown. "Look, as soon as I've gotten you to the lodge, I'll call him. At least then I'll know you're okay. By then, his team should be in place, and they can take over."

Micah's gaze consulted the rearview mirror as he spoke, watching out for trouble. Looking out for her, as he had from the day they met.

She couldn't doubt him, not now. "Okay," she said.

He shot a look at her. "Really? You're not going to run to any more truckers with a wild story?"

"I promise." She mimed crossing her heart. "Was it really such a bad thing? I mean, it turned out all right, didn't it?"

"I hope." He reached out, flicking on the CB radio on the dash. "The danger is that they'll talk. If the chatter reaches the wrong ears…"

He let that die away, but she understood. She'd made his job harder. She'd put them in more danger. If the bad guys caught up to them, it would be her fault.

Micah's prayers seem to be falling into a pattern—a plea to be assured that he was doing the right thing for Jade. He'd acted on instinct, but hadn't the events proved him right? If he hadn't reached the hotel garage when he did, Jade would be dead.

The stark thought was an icy hand around his heart.

No more second-guessing. He'd acted, and now he'd deal with the consequences. Fortunately, so far the chatter on the radio was mostly about the weather.

It was worsening, of course. What else could he expect on a wintry January day in Montana? Flakes had been drifting down from a concrete-gray sky for the past half hour, but now they seemed to be getting denser by the moment.

Protect us, Father. I don't see what else to do but this.

"The snow is getting worse." Jade pressed one hand against the dash as she leaned forward to peer through the windshield. "I should be getting used to this by now, but I haven't."

"Pittsburgh gets its share of snow, doesn't it?"

"Not like this. Anyway, in the city there's always a building to break up the scenery. You don't get this expanse of white, stretching so far you can't see where the road ends." She rubbed her arms, as if just looking at the snow made her cold.

"Staying on the road can be a matter of instinct." He smiled, hoping to reassure her. "Or maybe dumb luck."

"If I rely on that…"

He cut her off with a raised hand, zeroing in on the radio. His gut clenched as he listened to the chatter. Some trucker, probably bored with staring into endless snow-flakes, was recounting the episode at the truck stop. Others chimed in. Jaw hard, he snapped it off.

"I'm sorry. It's my fault."

Jade sounded so dismayed that he couldn't summon up any annoyance that things had turned out exactly as he'd feared.

"Forget it. Things happen, and we deal with them." He smiled, hearing his father's voice in his memory. "My dad used to say that to every misfortune, from a glass of spilled milk to a wrecked car. It's not a bad piece of ad-vice to live by, I've always thought."

"If they find us because of what I did…" She let that trail off, her fingers closing into fists on her knees.

He might have known she wouldn't let it go that easily. "Hey, take it easy. It was actually a very enlightening ex-perience. I enjoyed seeing Jade the librarian turn into Jade the actress. I didn't know you had it in you."

"I didn't, either." Her hands relaxed a little at his light-hearted tone. "I've never done anything like that before. Too shy, or maybe too much of a coward. Ruby…Ruby wouldn't hesitate to make a scene."

"True." He and Ruby had clashed loudly a couple of times when he was getting her settled. "Just because the two of you looked alike, it doesn't necessarily follow that you'd have the same personality."

"Do you think you're like your brother?"

The question slipped under his guard. Ordinarily he'd deflect questions about Jackson with a quip, but Jade was different. He wanted to let her in.

"In some ways, I guess. Choice of profession, to name the obvious. And we both look a bit like our father. Otherwise…well, it's sometimes seemed to me that we are about as different as could be." He darted a glance at Jade, to find her eyes focused on him intently. "He operates on rules and logic. You should like that."

"You follow your instincts. Your heart." Given the warmth of her voice, it didn't sound as if she had any desire to swap him out with his brother.

"I'm not sure…." His gaze flickered to the rearview mirror, and his breath hitched. For miles and miles there hadn't been another vehicle on the road. Now a pair of headlights pierced the thickening snow.

"What is it?" Jade swiveled, her eyes widening at the sight of the headlamps behind them.

"It could be anybody," he said quickly, but dread was pooling in his gut. The spacing and height of the headlamps told him it was probably a sedan. Even as he watched, the vehicle sped up, closing on them.

He focused on the road ahead, trying to see beyond the swirling flakes. "Keep an eye on them. Let me know if they get any closer."

"Right." She sounded calm, but her hand gripped the edge of the seat until her knuckles were white.

He accelerated cautiously, checking the screen of his GPS system, hoping to spot an exit.

"They're closer." Stress put an edge to Jade's voice. "It's the maroon sedan."

"Okay." He reached out to squeeze her hand quickly. "Make sure your seat belt is tight. I'll try to stay ahead of them enough to get off at the next exit. We can't lose them on the interstate."

His hands gripped the wheel, and he squinted into the snow. It was getting close to a whiteout. Any sensible driver would slow down in this, but the car behind them grew rapidly closer.

They'd be on his bumper in a few more minutes. He pressed the gas, feeling the tires bite into the snow. His truck might be old, but it was solid. The guy behind him was either supremely confident of his driving ability or a total idiot. He was still closing.

Murmuring a silent prayer, he accelerated, dividing his attention between the road ahead and the rearview mirror. If he went off the road, he and Jade would be done for. The sedan loomed in the mirror like an animal springing on its prey.

And then the lights swerved crazily. He held his breath, watching in the mirror as the driver struggled to regain control. The sedan spun for a long moment, skating across the road. Then it smashed into a snowbank.

"They're off the road."

"Thank You, God."

Jade's soft murmur touched his heart. He looked at the GPS screen.

"They could get back on the road again fairly quickly, depending on what damage they've done. We can't take a chance. There's an exit ramp coming up. We can get off there and hope the snow hides our tracks."

"Are there any towns? Any place where we can get help?"

"Afraid not." He tried to quell the worry that roiled within him. If he was making the wrong decision, he was risking Jade's life.

"It's okay." Jade seemed to be reading his thoughts. "I trust your judgment, Micah."

He nodded, the lump in his throat making speech impossible.

The exit lane opened up in front of them, unplowed but passable. Murmuring a silent prayer, he took the ramp.

The two-lane side road was as snow-covered as the interstate. Trees crowded close on either side, their dark green shadows giving a respite from the endless white.

He spared a glance for the mirror. "I don't see anything."

Jade turned in her seat, peering behind them. "Maybe we've lost them."

"We can hope." He wasn't willing to grant that entirely, but the thought encouraged him.

Maybe he was going to make this work. It wasn't really that far to the lodge, and once he had Jade safe—

Black ice. He knew it as soon as he hit it, but that was already too late. The vehicle spun crazily, the wheels searching for traction where there was none. He steered into the skid, fighting to regain control, but it was impossible, the road was like a malevolent entity, gobbling them up.

A tree loomed ahead of them. They slid toward it. He fought the wheel, trying to avoid it, but he couldn't, they were going to hit—

Jade—his thoughts reached out to her. They hit in an explosion of sound, and everything went black.

THIRTEEN

Jade pressed herself upright in the seat, trying to make sense of what had happened. She stared at a jagged star pattern for a moment before realizing it was the shattered windshield.

The truck—they'd slid on the ice. They'd hit a tree. Micah—

She tried to turn toward him. Pain shot through her knees. Her breath catching, she forced herself to look at Micah.

He slumped forward, as still as death. Blood dripped down over the steering wheel. Her heart thundered against her ribs as she unfastened her seat belt and scooted closer to him.

"Micah, are you all right?" Stupid question. Obviously he wasn't all right. She reached toward him, almost afraid to touch him.

Lord, protect him. Show me what to do. If You hear me, show me what to do.

She grasped his shoulders, then reconsidered and braced his head with one hand as she moved him away from the steering column. He slumped back against the seat. Blood ran down his face from a cut in his forehead, and his eyes were closed.

He was alive. She pressed her fingers against his throat,

memories of her most recent first-aid class jumbling in her mind. His skin was warm and the pulse thudded reassuringly.

Get the bleeding stopped, that was the first priority, wasn't it? Obviously no one was going to come along and help them. She was on her own.

She took a moment to assess herself. She must have cracked her knees on the dashboard when they hit, a reminder of the fact that the truck was too old to have airbags. She'd undoubtedly have plenty of bruises tomorrow, but everything seemed to be working. Micah wasn't so fortunate.

"You're going to be fine." She turned, rummaging in the backseat for something to stop the bleeding. Reassure the patient. Never mind if your own nerves were screaming. "Just a cut on your head, that's all."

Was that all? He had lost consciousness, and that couldn't be good. And she wouldn't know if anything else hurt him unless—until—he woke.

Her groping fingers touched a duffel bag, and she pulled it toward her. It was a gym bag, maybe, packed for a workout. She yanked out a white T-shirt and wadded it up.

Holding his head steady, she pressed the shirt against the cut. The bleeding had already slowed in the time it had taken to find a compress, and now his lack of consciousness worried her more than anything.

"Micah!" she said his name sharply. "Micah, wake up. Do you hear me?"

He groaned. His dark eyelashes flickered against his skin.

"That's right, come on, wake up. We were in an accident. I need you to wake up."

She knew only too well that panic edged her voice, and she tried to suppress it. They were alone, miles from anywhere, snow falling thickly around them. She could well imagine being stuck there until someone uncovered them in the spring thaw.

"Micah, wake up! I need you."

"Don't…shout." His voice was a husky whisper, but it sounded comfortingly annoyed. "What happened?" His eyes opened, and he seemed to make an effort to keep them that way.

"We slid off the road and hit a tree. Micah, talk to me."

But his eyes had closed again, and a slight frown was the only response.

She had to get help. Holding the pad on his forehead with one hand, she reached out with the other and snagged the strap of her handbag, pulling it toward her. She yanked out her cell phone and flipped it open.

Nothing. Not a single bar showed. They really were in the middle of nowhere.

Micah had used the radio to listen to the truckers. That meant he could talk on it, didn't it? Hampered by her ignorance, she fumbled with it to no avail. She slapped her hand against the dash.

"I can't get the radio to work. Or the cell phone. I guess we're on our own." She was talking as much for her benefit as his, trying to stave off panic. "I'm going to try to start the truck, but I'll have to move you to do that."

Gently, she took the pad away from the cut and let out a relieved sigh. The bleeding had slowed to a sluggish trickle. He might need stitches, but at least he wasn't going to bleed to death.

More likely freeze to death. If she couldn't get the car started and get some heat for them...

Well, no sense in thinking about the worst. "You're going to have to help me, Micah."

No response. She'd have to do it herself. *Give me strength, Lord.*

Thankful for her boots and wool slacks, she zipped her jacket and shoved open the door on her side. She slid out, sinking into the snow nearly to the tops of her boots. Dense flakes blew in her face and stuck to her hair. She pulled her hood up and made her way around the 4x4, squinting through the driving snow to assess the situation.

It could be worse. They weren't too far off the road and were nearly level with its surface. If the vehicle would start, she ought to be able to get it back on the road. If.

First things first. She had to get Micah out of the driver's seat before she could do anything. She opened his door and climbed up next to him.

It wouldn't be easy to get him over the center console and into the other seat, even if he could help, and at the moment, he lolled back, boneless as a rag doll. She unhooked his seat belt, slid her arm under his and attempted to lift him toward the other seat.

Minutes later she was sweating in spite of the cold, and she hadn't moved him an inch. She bit her lip. She'd never get it done without his help.

"Micah!" She grabbed his shoulder and shook him gently. "Wake up. You have to help me."

This time when his eyes opened they seemed to focus. A gleam of intelligence encouraged her. "Jade."

"Right. Jade. Come on, you have to help me. You need to move into the other seat so I can start the car." His eyes began to drift shut, and she shook him again. "Don't do that. Keep your eyes open. Whatever you do, keep your eyes open."

He lifted his hand to his head, and she stopped it before he could touch the cut. He grimaced. "Banged myself up. You okay?"

"I'm fine. Nothing but a few bruises. Do you think you can slide over to the other seat?"

"I'll try," he muttered. He reached toward the seat, raising himself a couple of inches before slumping back again. "Dizzy. Wait a sec." He grabbed the steering wheel, levering himself with it.

He wasn't going to make it. She slid her arm around him, took as much of his weight on her as she could. "On three, okay?"

He managed a nod.

"One, two." She took a breath. "Three."

She heaved. He pulled. His jacket snagged on the gearshift, and she yanked it free. Somehow, between them, they got him into the other seat. He leaned back, white and sweating. Blood trickled down his forehead again.

"I'm sorry. Your head probably needs stitches. I shouldn't have tried to make you move." But what else could she have done?

"S'okay. Did right." He shut his eyes for a second, but he didn't lose consciousness. "First-aid kit. In the back."

Encouraged, she crawled behind the seats, finding the first-aid kit, along with a blanket, water, matches and candle, standard kit for driving in a Montana winter. She slid back into the front, dropping her bounty between them, and ripped open an antiseptic packet.

She leaned across him to swab off the cut, bracing herself on the seat to keep from putting her weight on him. He winced at her inexpert care, but he didn't make a sound. Quickly she dabbed on first-aid cream and put on a butterfly bandage. She surveyed it doubtfully.

"Maybe I should…"

He pushed her hand away. "It's fine." He sounded fretful. "Just get us back on the road."

"I'll try."

She turned the key, uttering a silent prayer. Amazingly enough, the motor caught on the first effort. The truck might be old, but Micah probably kept it perfectly maintained.

Now… She peered back over her shoulder. The road was there somewhere, obscured by the swirling snow. If she went straight back, they should hit it.

She struggled to get the shift into Reverse. Stepped on the gas. And heard the wheels spin frantically, probably digging them deeper into the snow.

Micah braced himself, sitting upright with an effort that made his lips tighten. "Rock it," he said. "Go forward, then back, quick as you can."

She shoved the stubborn gearshift. It had been too long since she'd driven a vehicle with a stick shift. She was spoiled, that was all. Why couldn't she do such a simple thing now, when their safety depended on it?

Micah watched, frowning as if it was an effort to focus. He was probably thinking that he could do it much better himself.

"It's no use." She pounded the steering wheel. "I can't do it."

"Sure you can. Give it another try."

He wasn't giving up. She couldn't, either.

Another rock, another failure. The wheels spun in the snow. Try again. Again, sending up a despairing prayer.

Finally she got the knack of it. The wheels caught. Euphoria surged through her as the vehicle shot backward onto the road, jolting to a stop when she hit the brake.

"We did it."

"You did it." His lips lifted in a faint smile. "Good work."

She wanted to stop time right there, to enjoy the moment of shared triumph, but she couldn't. For all they knew, their pursuers could be right behind them. They couldn't call for help, and the snow fell as thickly as ever.

"We should get going." She put the vehicle in gear and heard an ominous mutter from the engine. "That doesn't sound good."

"It'll get us there. Always been reliable." His eyes drifted shut, and he seemed to force them open. "Don't let me go to sleep."

"I won't," she promised. "No matter what."

She nursed the 4x4 down the snowy road, peering into swirling whiteness, trying to keep them in the faint depressions that marked another vehicle's passage. She talked, asked questions, talked nonsense, anything to keep Micah awake.

She talked about anything and everything except the important thing, the thing that filled her heart and mind with astonishment. Somehow, during those moments when their safety hung in the balance, she'd recognized the truth.

She loved him. She loved Micah with all her heart.

She had no idea what he felt for her. She didn't know whether they'd even live long enough to make it matter. But at the moment they were here, together, alive. That was all she cared about.

* * *

Micah's mind finally started to clear. He turned toward Jade. A wave of dizziness hit, so that for an instant he thought the vehicle was spinning on ice again. He braced his hand against the dash until the spinning stopped.

"What's wrong?" Jade's concern reached out to touch him, even though she didn't take her eyes from the road ahead.

"Nothing." He hated admitting weakness, but if they were going to survive this, he better be honest. "A little dizzy when I move my head, that's all."

"You need to be seen by a doctor." Jade's hands were so tense on the wheel that her fingers were bone-white.

"No chance of that right now. Anyway, I'll be okay. I've had worse hits than this on a high school football field and gone right back in."

"You probably lied to the coach and told him you were fine."

"I probably did. Teenage boys can be pretty dumb about things like that. Too busy trying to be macho to think straight."

"Well, don't go all macho on me now." She swung a quick glance at him before riveting her gaze to the road again. "Be honest about it."

"I'll be honest with you about everything, Jade." That was a pretty big statement for a man in his line of work, but he meant every word. "I promise."

"Thank you." Her voice went husky on the words.

"So, even though I'd like to insist on taking the wheel, I won't, since I'm seeing double every time I move my head."

Talking was helping, though. It seemed to speed up his sluggish mental processes.

"I'd be happy to be able to see just one road at this point." Every line in Jade's body was tense. "I keep feeling as if I could go off the berm and not even know it."

"You're doing fine." He longed to soothe the tension from her neck and shoulders, but he didn't dare touch her. Neither of them could stand the distraction right now. Instead he reached for the GPS, tilting it so that he could see the screen. Nothing.

"I'm afraid that's what you hit your head on," Jade said.

"Looks like it didn't do either of us much good." A glance at the radio told him that wasn't an option. He fumbled in his pocket for his cell phone.

"I tried mine when…when you weren't coming round." There was a telltale tremor in her voice. "I couldn't get a signal."

He'd scared her, in other words. She'd been in trouble, and he'd been out cold.

He turned his on. "Not much here, either, but I'll give it a try." He punched in Jackson's cell number.

It seemed to take forever. Finally he heard the faint sound of a connection, but the call went straight to voice mail. Better than nothing.

"Micah here. We're on the road paralleling I-90, trying to get Jade to Stan Guthrie up at Black Creek Lodge. She'll be safe there until you can arrange protection." He hoped he didn't sound as worried as he felt. Hoped Jackson would get this. "The shooters in the maroon sedan from the parking garage were on our tail, but I think we've lost them. I'll contact you when we get there." He clicked off in a haze of static.

"Did it go through?"

He read the fear in her voice. "I think so. When he gets

it..." he wouldn't say *if*. Jade was spooked enough already "...he'll probably send a backup team straight to the lodge to meet us. Meanwhile, let's just look on the bright side."

"And that would be?" A little of the spirit came back into her words.

"Well, we're alive. And we haven't seen anything of our followers for miles. We'll have to hope they're still sitting out there on the interstate, waiting for a tow."

"Being alive is definitely a high point." Her tension seemed to ease a bit. "There were moments when I had my doubts, especially when I saw that tree coming at us."

The memory swept over him, and he couldn't maintain the light tone. "I'm sorry, Jade. It's my fault you're in this situation. I thought..."

"Just stop." She sent him a look that was nearly a glare. "Don't you apologize to me for trying to keep me alive. I won't listen to that. Okay?"

"Okay." He wouldn't persist when she so clearly didn't want to hear it. If he had doubts, he'd keep them to himself.

He'd been wrong about Jade too often. That first day he'd thought her rigid and uncaring, and that had colored his dealings with her.

Now...now he knew her. Now he understood the courage and tenacity that dwelt behind that beautiful exterior and that prim manner. Those were qualities he admired in anyone, but in Jade, in went beyond that. Far beyond that.

He cared. Cared deeply...deeply enough to risk his job, his future, his life for her.

Love. He let his mind circle around the word cautiously, unwilling to admit to it. Then he pushed it away. Whatever he felt for Jade, it would have to wait. Right now the only important thing was her safety. He didn't dare let his emotions get the better of him when her life was at stake.

And if he was going to keep from betraying his feelings, he had to steer away from saying anything personal. He sucked in a breath, realizing he'd been quiet too long. She'd be thinking…well, he wasn't sure what. He just knew he had to be careful, or he'd fall so hard for her that all of his professional skill might just vanish in a whirlwind of emotion.

"I guess…" He paused, cleared his throat. "We haven't really talked enough about what's going on as far as the case is concerned."

"We've been a little busy." The trace of a smile touched her face. "You don't have to tell me anything that you're not supposed to. I trust you."

"Thanks, but in this situation I think the time for professional discretion has passed." He tried to arrange the thoughts in his mind. "I was out of the office this morning in order to meet with a woman who is in hiding until it's time for her to testify against Vincent Martino. The Martino crime family from Chicago. You know about them?"

Her forehead wrinkled. "Vaguely. There was something on the news lately about a Mafia don in Chicago who was critically ill. Is that the one?"

"That's Vincent's father. Word is out that Vincent is trying to pay a final tribute to his father. We think the tribute is killing a woman who put his father in jail years ago. Apparently the Mob knows that the woman is supposedly living somewhere in Montana."

"Somewhere?" She caught the salient point. "You mean they don't know where or you don't know where?"

"She was in witness protection, but she left." He sifted through what he'd learned from Jackson about Kristin Perry's birth mother. That part of it wasn't his to tell.

"Okay," she said slowly, sounding as if she were doing some sifting, too. "Even if we assume they're after me because they're not sure whether I'm Jade or Ruby, I still don't see what that has to do with Ruby. She'd never even been to Chicago."

"That's the part that had us confused, too. But it's beginning to look as if Vincent Martino put out a contract on the woman. No one knows much about her, but they do know that her last known address was in Montana. And that she has green eyes. And that she's in the Witness Protection Program."

"But that...that's ridiculous." Jade's logical mind rejected that instantly. "Even if they are thugs, they can't be stupid enough to go around killing every green-eyed woman in Montana who's under protection."

"Never underestimate the stupidity of the average bad guy. If they were Einsteins, we wouldn't catch as many as we do."

"Even so..."

"I know. But two women who were in Witness Protection in Montana have been killed. Both had green eyes. And now they're making a concerted effort to kill you."

It sounded unlikely, even put that way.

"Look, I'd dismiss it as coincidence, except that someone's gone to a lot of trouble to bribe or threaten the locations of those women out of a federal employee. And there's another thing. That woman...the one they're trying to kill...her name is Eloise."

He saw that hit. Her green eyes widened as she took her gaze from the road for an instant.

"That was the name that man called me. The one at the library."

"Right. That's what put us on to it. My brother is convinced that there's an open contract out on Eloise. That means that anyone can kill her and claim the reward."

"So there are a bunch of armed maniacs roaming around Montana."

He grimaced. "I wouldn't exactly put it that way. Vincent Martino is no dummy, from everything I've learned about him and his organization." His thoughts flickered toward the endless files and photographs he'd scanned through after that initial memo from Jackson about the Martino crime family. "He can't be happy that his goons are drawing attention to themselves."

"If that's so, then once he realizes that I'm not the woman he's after, he'll leave me alone." Her voice lifted, as if she saw her way through the dark.

He wanted to encourage her. She deserved to have a little hope at this point. But once Martino had set this bloody rampage into motion, how would it end? Two women were dead already.

Not Jade next. *Please, God, not Jade.*

"We've got to hope so." He tried to infuse optimism into the words. "And to keep you safe until then."

As if it had heard his words and despaired, the engine died.

FOURTEEN

Black despair settled on Micah. He fought it off. He couldn't let himself think that way. They weren't done for yet.

Jade shot him a wide-eyed glance. Then she turned the key. The engine answered with a trembling death rattle.

"Don't bother. I'm afraid that's it. Poor old lady never let me down before."

"Are you talking about me or the car?"

Jade's question was pure bravado, but he was glad to hear it. She wouldn't give up easily.

"The 4x4, definitely."

"What do we do now?"

He frowned through the windshield at the road ahead. The snow was finally slacking off, but it lay a foot deep and untracked on the macadam. He weighed the options, not liking any of them.

"Conventional wisdom says to stay with the vehicle, keep warm, wait for help. But this isn't an ordinary situation. With the engine dead, it's going to be as cold inside as it is outside in a matter of minutes."

"You have an emergency kit. I've always heard you

should light the candle and wrap up in blankets until someone comes."

He eyed her thoughtfully. Jade was reasonably fit, but she was no athlete. To tramp through the snow took strength.

"We haven't seen a single vehicle come down this road since we've been on it. I'd say the chances of someone coming along to help aren't too great. And if someone does come along, it might be the people we want least to see."

She took a breath as that unpalatable truth sank in. "You think we should start walking."

She obviously didn't want to.

"Let's have a look at the map first and figure out where we are." He reached across her to yank a highway map from the pocket next to the driver's seat, flipping it open.

He traced the map with his finger, and she leaned close to watch. Soft curls brushed his cheek, distracting him until he dragged his thoughts back to the problem at hand.

"This is where we were before the accident." He ran his finger along the winding gray line. "I'm guessing we've gotten maybe twenty miles since then." He tapped the map. "We haven't reached that crossroads, that's for sure. And it's an access road that leads to the interstate, so there ought to be traffic on it."

"How far do you think it is?"

"Maybe a couple of miles." Maybe farther, but there was no point in discouraging her.

She glanced up at him, her face so close that his breath hitched. Worry darkened her eyes. "Do you really think you can make it that far? Your head…"

She was afraid for him, not for herself. Emotion gripped his throat, and he tried to speak normally.

"I'm fine. A brisk walk on a winter day will do me good."

"I doubt that." But her expression lightened at his reaction, so he must have been convincing. "Well, let's get going."

"Not so fast. Preparation is half the battle." He turned to reach behind the seat, trying to ignore a wave of dizziness. "Let's see what's here that we can use."

It took some maneuvering in the close confines of the vehicle, but he pulled his duffel bag and backpack into the front with them.

"I'm not putting on your sweatpants," she warned. "And I've already used your T-shirt on your forehead."

"What do you say to a University of Chicago sweatshirt? Frayed but clean." He held it out.

She shook her head. "I'm fine. You put it on."

She was still trying to take care of him. He appreciated it even as it irked him. "This parka of mine is good to thirty below. You need the extra layer more than I do."

Her fingers closed over the sweatshirt reluctantly, but at a stern glance from him she dragged it on over her head. She pulled on her jacket, struggling a bit in the confined space against the steering wheel until he grabbed the hood and pulled it into place, his fingers brushing her cheek.

Oddly reluctant to let go, he tucked her wool muffler carefully around her neck, taking an unnecessary amount of time. "You have a hat and gloves, I hope. That'll keep your head warmer than just a hood." His voice was husky.

"In my pocket." Hers sounded just as husky.

He lingered a moment longer. Then, giving in to temptation, he kissed her lips. Lightly, very lightly. But even so, he felt the impact shoot straight to his heart.

He pulled back, fighting for control, and busied himself checking the contents of the backpack. "I have water and a few energy bars. You want one before we start?"

"Not right now."

She had to be hungry, but there was no point in making an issue of it. They might be glad of those bars later, when the extra calories could keep them going a bit farther.

"Let's go, then." He opened the door and slid out into the road, feeling the cold bite into him.

Jade followed suit.

Please let this be the right decision. He'd been acting on instinct all along, and he didn't know whether to trust it or not. But if he hadn't trusted it earlier, Jade would have been lying dead in that hotel parking garage back in Billings.

"We'll have to walk on the road, even if we're more visible that way. If we get off into the snow, we won't have to worry about the bad guys or anything else."

She fell into step with him, glancing at the snowy woods on either side of the road. A shiver went through her. "This is not a place where I'd like to be lost."

Obviously he shouldn't talk about all the things that could go wrong. Realizing she was trying to keep pace with him, Micah shortened his stride.

"So." He blew out a steamy breath. "Once this is all over, what will you do?" Keep her focused on the future, not on the icy present.

"Do?" She looked startled. "Go back to my job, of course. Assuming they'll have me."

"I thought maybe you'd have developed a distaste for Montana after all you've been through."

"Never. I love it here, cold and all. It's the first place I've ever lived where I really feel as if I belong."

"That's good to hear. On behalf of my adopted state, I appreciate the fact that you're calling it home."

She frowned down at the snow that dragged at their feet. "Home," she said softly, her breath coming raggedly. "I've never had one before. I don't want to lose it."

He wrapped his hand around hers. "You won't. Not if I can help it."

She nodded, and he suspected she didn't have enough breath left to carry on a conversation. To tell the truth, he wasn't doing so well himself. Maybe it was the head injury, but his limbs seemed to weigh hundreds of pounds.

Shaking off the thought, he kept moving. They were all right as long as they kept moving. No walk in the park, but he was fit. He could do it.

Twenty minutes of slogging through the snow later, he wasn't so sure. It was all he could do to keep putting one foot in front of the other. And Jade looked as if she was walking in a dream. Or maybe a nightmare.

He stared down the road. No signs. No indication of habitation. How far were they from that crossroads? Did they stand a chance at all of making it?

Please, Father. Give us strength. Send us help.

"Are you praying?" Jade's voice was a whisper, carried on the cold air.

"Yeah." Were they on the same wavelength?

"Me, too."

"I'm glad." He squeezed her hand, thinking of all she'd revealed about her spiritual struggles. "Remember Elijah and the ravens?"

"Vaguely," she said

"They brought help didn't they? We could." *Please, Father.*

A few more steps, and Jade stopped moving. She bent over, hands on her knees, breathing hard. "Just a minute's rest. That's all."

At least she was on her feet, not sinking down into the snow. "Just a minute." He put his arm around her, supporting her. His heart twisted with concern.

Then he heard a sound, breaking the smothered silence of the snowy woods. An engine. Someone was coming.

He swung, looking back the way they'd come. He loosened his jacket, reaching for his weapon. If it was the maroon sedan...

It wasn't. He eased his hand away from his weapon and raised his arms to flag down the driver.

The pickup was so old that it was impossible to tell what its original color had been. Mostly rust, now, but it couldn't be in as bad shape as it looked. It came grinding through the snow and pulled to a stop next to them.

The driver was considerably older than the truck, her leathery face a mass of wrinkles. Wiry gray hair made a fringe around a battered Stetson. She lowered the window a cautious couple of inches, and a pair of bright blue eyes surveyed them.

"Looks like you folks been having some trouble."

"We went off the road a ways back." He'd identify himself if he had to, but he'd rather they remain anonymous. "I guess we shouldn't have gotten off the interstate."

"I got no use for them interstates. Bunch of fools going nowhere too fast."

"Maybe so." He suspected that was a shotgun tucked down beside the seat. She wasn't being too quick to trust, and he didn't blame her. "We're on our way to visit a friend up near Helena. Any chance you can give us a lift to someplace where we can make a call?"

She surveyed them for a moment longer. Then she jerked a nod. "Hop in. I'll take you as far as I'm going, anyway."

He opened the door, helping Jade up into the seat and climbing in after her.

Thank You, Lord. We'll take ravens in any form when sent by You.

Heat blasted from the truck's dash, but Jade couldn't seem to stop shivering, even tucked between their rescuer and Micah's solid body. Maybe she just hadn't been able to feel how cold she was until relief had come.

She stretched hands and feet toward the source of all that heat. The truck's cab was cramped and a little smelly, but it felt great.

"That's right. You just get yourself warmed up now." The elderly woman's voice sounded rusty, as if she didn't have much use for it. "What's your name?"

"Jade."

Micah shot her a sidelong warning look, and she knew what he was telling her as clearly as if he had spoken. *Don't tell her what's going on. Don't say anything you don't have to.*

After that disaster with the truckers, she'd follow his advice.

"My name is Micah." He reached across her to shake

hands with the woman. "We're grateful to you for giving us a lift."

"Mamie Carson." She gave a sound that could only be described as a snort. "Couldn't leave you out there to freeze to death, could I?"

"We're fortunate you came along, Ms. Carson." Micah shifted a bit, his arm going around Jade's shoulders so that she felt the comforting weight of it.

"Never mind thanks. You'd best get your girl's hands warmed up. She oughta have warmer gloves than that. Mittens work best of anything." She flapped a pair of oversized fur-lined mittens that lay in her lap.

Most of the time Jade didn't care for that use of the word *girl* applied to her, but this use of it warmed her. Micah's girl.

He drew her gloves off carefully and wrapped his hands around hers. "You should have told me your hands were getting this bad." His tone was intimate, gently scolding. "I'd have given you my gloves."

"Then you'd have frost-bitten fingers, which wouldn't help us at all." She tried to make the words tart to override the treacherous melting that his touch engendered.

"Rub 'em real easy," Mamie cautioned. "Don't want to be rough."

"I won't be." He massaged her fingers, the movements as tender as a kiss.

"Here." Mamie reached behind her seat and pulled out a plaid blanket, dropping it on Jade's lap. "Put that over you 'til you warm up."

The blanket was rough and frayed, and it smelled like horse. She wrapped it around herself thankfully. "Thanks. I think I'm actually starting to feel my hands and feet."

"Good." Micah shot her a look that would warm her all by itself. "I was getting worried."

"I reckon Jade's tougher than that." Mamie elbowed her. "Right?"

The old woman's question seemed to demand an honest answer.

"I'm trying to be."

Ruby had always been the tough one. Jade had told herself she didn't have to take that path—that she could rely on intelligence and hard work. Maybe she'd never appreciated toughness enough. Mamie Carson certainly seemed like an example of that.

"You live out here, do you, Ms. Carson?" Micah asked, looking up from his focus on Jade's hands.

"Got a little spread down near the crossroads. Born there and gonna die there, if I have my way."

Near the crossroads. That meant they'd have to climb out there and walk toward the interstate, hoping to pick up another ride. Her heart failed at the thought of getting out into the cold again.

Nonsense. She'd do what she had to do.

"Are you on the telephone, by chance?" Micah's tone sharpened.

"Nope. Never saw much need for it. I guess the phone company never did neither. Never ran the lines out. Some folks have those fancy cell phones, but I hear tell they don't work so good out here."

Micah pulled his out of his pocket and flipped it open. He shook his head. "I see what you mean. I'm not getting a signal."

So they couldn't count on getting help anytime soon. She bit her lip, studying Micah's face. It was pale, and there were lines of strain around his eyes and mouth. How much longer could he keep going? He ought to be in an E.R. getting checked out.

He wouldn't give up or give in, no matter how much he hurt. But his body might overcome his indomitable will.

"Here's my lane." Mamie pulled the truck to the side of the road, nosing into a lane that was nearly invisible in the snow. "There's the road you want just ahead. Turn left, and it'll get you onto the highway in about a mile or so."

Micah let go of her hands. "We thank you for the lift, Ms. Carson."

"Hold on there. You think I'm just gonna desert the two of you?" Mamie's leathery face cracked in a smile. "I know folks in trouble when I see them. Reckon I know good folks from bad, too. You two take the truck and get on your way."

She was already sliding out before either of them found words.

"We can't do that. What will you do for transportation?" Bless her heart—they couldn't leave her alone out here, either.

"I've got a horse that's as reliable as this old truck any day." Mamie pulled a couple of canvas bags out of the back, taking one in each hand. "Got all the groceries I need now for a long spell. I'll do what I do every winter— hole up and wait for spring."

"We appreciate it, but we can't let you do that." Micah said the words in his best authoritative cop voice.

It didn't seem to impress the woman. "You just heed what I say. You'll bring the truck back when you don't need it anymore. Till then, you take care of this girl."

She didn't wait for an answer or an argument. She

turned and stomped off down the lane. Jade watched until the incongruous figure vanished around a stand of trees.

"What are we going to do?"

Micah slid out and walked around the truck, climbing into the driver's seat. Then he gave her a singularly sweet smile. "We're going to take what's offered. You have to admit it. When the good Lord decides to send help, He does it right."

Micah put the pickup in gear and pulled out. Amazing, how fast things could turn around. A half hour ago, he'd been wondering how they'd survive. Now he was buoyed by a sense of optimism.

"Okay, now things are going our way." He made the turn toward the interstate. "We'll get back on the highway. Even with slow going from the snow, we'll be at the lodge in a couple of hours."

"It can't be that easy." Jade sounded as if she didn't quite believe in their change of fortunes.

"Why not? We've had enough bad things happen to us." They were coming up on the interstate ramp already, and he took it. No cars in sight, but tracks in the snow told him some traffic was moving.

"I hope you're right." A smile wiped some of the worry from Jade's eyes. "Ms. Carson was a dear, wasn't she?"

"Tough, self-reliant, open-handed to those needing help. That's the best of folks out here."

"You'll never go back to Chicago?"

"Not unless I get reassigned, which I hope doesn't happen."

"Don't you have people there any longer?"

"Just my brother." His gut tightened at the thought of

Jackson's current opinion of him. "My mom lives in Phoenix. I'm settled here now."

"It's good, isn't it? Feeling settled."

Jade had good reason to feel that way, based on everything she'd told him. "You know it." He reached out to clasp her hand. "You'll be back in your own house soon. Everything will be the way it was. Well, except for your bells. I guess you'll have to start a new collection."

Her hand jerked in his, as if in denial.

"I'm sorry," he said quickly. "I didn't mean to bring up a sore subject."

"It's all right." She was silent for a moment, but her hand relaxed a bit in his. "I told you the bells didn't mean anything special. That wasn't true."

"I sort of figured that." Was she actually going to confide in him?

"I told you about my librarian friend, Mrs. Henderson. I stayed with her once—it was a rough time, and she just let me go home with her." Jade's voice filled with a kind of wonder, as if that sort of kindness hadn't happened often in her young life.

"That was good of her."

"Yes. She was a good person, good all the way through."

He knew what she meant by the phrase. Most people had some little quirks—the odd touchy places that made them get defensive, or lie, or cheat in some way to protect themselves. Some few were good all the way through. His mother was one of those.

"She had a little house in a nice neighborhood, with everything as neat and orderly as her library. She had a collection of bells that she'd bought when she traveled.

She had a story about every one of them." Jade's hands moved, as if they tried to express something for which she didn't have words. "I guess that became my image of a home I'd have one day, where everything was clean and neat, and you could have something fragile without it being broken."

"That made it hurt doubly to see yours broken." This was the explanation of her tears, and his throat went tight thinking of it.

"It was like…" she hesitated "…like being trapped in that world again." Her voice dropped on the words.

He could fill in the pieces. Her mother had been an alcoholic and an addict. Anything fragile or remotely valuable would have been broken or sold to support her habit.

"You're not there anymore," he said firmly, praying that what he said was true.

She nodded, but he wasn't sure she totally believed that. She was swinging back and forth between hope and despair, and that wasn't surprising, even what she'd been through today. Maybe the best thing he could do for her right now was to keep her talking.

"You said you stayed with her for a while. How did that happen?"

She didn't answer. Silence stretched between them. A semi went by in the passing lane, going too fast for road conditions and splattering the windshield with slush. The wipers struggled to clear the glass.

"I must have been about thirteen at the time." Jade clasped her hands together in her lap. "My mother…well, you know what she was like. There was always a boyfriend around. This one drank as much as she did. Usually when he was there I could stay out of his way."

"And that time?" He kept his voice soft with an effort, guessing what was coming.

"He came on to me." Her fingers strained against each other. "Maybe he'd just noticed that Ruby and I were growing up. Anyway, I panicked. I got away from him, but I knew I had to get out of there. Once Mom got high she wouldn't protect me."

Edie Summers had been a poor excuse for a mother, all right. Once he'd have denied that people like that existed, but his job had taught him better.

"So you left?" He longed to pull over so that he could give her his full attention, but he was afraid if he did that, it would break the thread of remembrance.

"I tried to get Ruby to go with me, but she just laughed. She insisted that when he got drunk he got generous. She called me a coward. So I left."

She was probably holding on to control by a thread, but he sensed that she needed to get this out. "Where did you go?"

"The library. I stayed until closing, and Ms. Henderson seemed to see what I didn't say." She let out a shaky breath. "I stayed a couple of days. When I went home, Ruby flashed a wad of cash. She insisted nothing had happened. Said he'd just given it to her."

"You didn't believe her." His heart seemed to be splitting in half at her pain.

"No." She breathed the word. "I didn't. Things were never the same between us after that."

"It wasn't your fault," he said, knowing that's what she believed. "You couldn't help what happened."

She swung her face toward him, and he saw that tears spilled over onto her cheeks. "I should have. I should have helped her. She was my sister. Maybe if I'd stayed..."

"If you'd stayed, you'd have been the one he raped," he said the words bluntly. Better to get it out in the open. "You tried to help her. She didn't let you."

Her breath hitched. "If I'd tried harder, maybe I could have gotten her to leave with me. Maybe she'd never have gone down the path she did. Maybe she'd be alive today."

"Maybe. And maybe a hundred other things might have been different."

Unable to stand it any longer, he pulled onto the berm and stopped, putting the truck's flashers on. Then he pulled her into his arms.

For an instant she strained against him. Then she turned her face into his shoulder and let the tears take over.

He'd held her like this before, when she'd wept after Ruby's funeral. He'd cared then. He'd wanted to comfort her.

Now...now she meant so much to him that his heart was breaking with it. He loved her. How had he not seen it before? How had he been able to deny it?

He loved her, and he could do nothing to ease her pain. Nothing but hold her, and stroke her hair and try to share her pain.

FIFTEEN

She had wept in his arms before. The thought shook Jade out of the fog of misery that gripped her. That time had been over Ruby. This…this was about her terrible guilt, and she didn't see how he could even want to comfort her, knowing how she'd let her sister down.

"It was my fault," she whispered the words, needing to make him understand.

"No." He drew back a little and took her face in his hands, cradling it. "Don't say that. It wasn't your fault. You were a kid, trying to survive. You couldn't make her go with you."

"I should have." She couldn't let go of it, and she knew with sudden clarity that this was what had come between her and God. How could God ever forgive this? "I should have found a way to help her. Instead I just saved myself."

"Stop it." He sounded almost angry, and his fingers tightened. "You did what you had to do."

"But…" She couldn't let go of her guilt so easily. She'd been living with it too long.

"No buts. Don't you see? Yes, a terrible thing happened that night. But there were lots of other times when

Ruby could have made different choices. She consistently made the one that she thought was easy."

"That's not fair. She didn't deserve what happened to her." She tried to pull away, but he wouldn't let her.

"Of course not. Neither of you deserved to be born into that situation." His gaze was intent on his face, burning into her. "This isn't about deserving. It's about choices. All along the way, Ruby made her own choices. It wasn't until the world crashed in on her that she finally made the hard one."

She stilled, thinking about that.

The hard grip of Micah's hands eased. His thumbs stroked her cheeks, wiping away the tears.

"Ruby wasn't you. She looked for a different way out. You couldn't change her any more than she could change you. But in the end..." He hesitated, as if searching for words. "In the end, she did the right thing. She found her way back to God."

He kissed her eyes, first one, then the other, in a touch so gentle it might have been a blessing. "We can't change the past. You don't know why she took the road she did, but she ended up where she belonged. She was content. I told you that, remember? I'm sure she had regrets, but she was content."

She had to ask the question that haunted her. "Do you think she forgave me?"

"I doubt she ever thought there was anything to forgive. You knew your sister. Do you think she'd welcome the idea that you were supposed to rescue her?"

That sliced through her misery like a knife, and she almost smiled. "She'd have been more likely to smack me if I suggested it."

"There you go, then." His eyes filled with so much ten-

derness that it took her breath away. "If there was anything to forgive, God forgave it long ago. You're the only
one who hasn't forgiven yourself."

The words seemed to sink into her heart, soothing
away all the pain she'd been hiding so carefully. Healing
her. Making her whole.

Micah stretched, bracing his hands against the steering
wheel. His head was no longer throbbing, just the posses-
sor of a dull ache that extended right down to his shoulders.

He glanced across the seat at Jade. She looked relaxed,
even half-asleep. She'd been better after they'd talked, as
if what he said really had helped.

Since then, they'd made one uneventful stop for food,
which they'd both desperately needed. Other than that,
he sensed that they'd both felt oddly at peace after those
moments when Jade had bared her soul to him.

They'd been close, closer than he ever had been to another person. If they got through this, he knew he wanted
her in his life.

Still, he had to be careful. He might be sure of his own
mind, but Jade was vulnerable. She'd gone through the
tragedy of her sister's death, narrowly escaped death herself, and had her world turned upside down. He couldn't
rush her or take advantage of her vulnerability.

And, always assuming he still had a job after this, he
ought to wait until the case cleared. Which could be a
long time, the way things had been going.

No, he couldn't believe that. The very fact that so much
had happened so quickly meant that Martino was rushing
into this without thinking. That made him prone to error, and
with Jackson on his case, Vincent couldn't afford errors.

Jade sat up, blinking. "I was nearly asleep. Is everything all right?"

"Fine. Traffic is starting to pick up."

There were more trucks on the road as the drivers tried to make up for whatever time they'd lost. The passing lanes were slush-covered, but otherwise the road wasn't too bad.

"It's getting dark." She pushed back her sleeve to check her watch. "Is it just me, or has this day lasted forever?"

"Definitely not just you, but it's nearly over. The next exit is ours." He frowned at the gray January dusk settling in. "It'll be dark by the time we get to the top of the mountain, though." He felt for his cell phone. "I'd better try Jackson again."

The faintest of signals, but maybe it would be enough. Someone picked up on the second ring, and he heard his brother's voice through a fog of static.

"Jackson, listen, we're almost to the lodge."

Jackson said something in response, but he stopped listening, focusing instead on the rearview mirror.

"We've picked up a tail again." He pressed the phone to his ear, praying he was getting through. "I have to lose them."

Jade swiveled in the seat, her eyes wide. "How did they find us? We're not even in the same vehicle."

"Worry about that later." He dropped the phone to grab the wheel with both hands and pressed the accelerator. "I've got to lose them. We can't risk leading them straight to the lodge."

"How?" She braced her hands against the seat as the truck surged forward. "There's no place to hide on the interstate."

They passed a sign. The exit was a mile ahead. Take it? He thought of the lonely, winding road that led up to the lodge.

The maroon sedan cut in front of a semi, earning a blast of the horn. Surely they wouldn't risk taking a shot in full view of several truck drivers. That hadn't deterred them so far, though.

The sedan was in the passing lane now, closing fast. No chance to lose them—

With a triumphant blare of the horn, the semi driver swung back in front of the sedan. For a moment, at least, they were hidden from the sedan driver's view, and there was the exit.

Holding his breath, Micah waited until the last possible second and slewed the wheel, sending them shrieking onto the exit ramp. The semi and the sedan rocketed past the exit while he slid his way down to the stop sign.

"You did it." Jade grasped his arm. "By the time they get to the next exit, we'll be safe."

"They may not be that obedient to traffic laws. Still, by the time they find a break in the guard rails where they can get turned around, we'll be halfway up the mountain." He took his hand off the wheel long enough to squeeze hers. "It's not long now. When we get to the lodge, we'll be safe."

The tires bit into the mix of snow and gravel on the side of the mountain road, jerking Micah to attention. He blinked, careful not to oversteer as he got them back into the ruts made by previous drivers.

"Are you all right?" Faint alarm sounded in Jade's voice. "Do you want me to drive?"

"I'm fine." He took his gaze off the road long enough

for a quick assessment. One look at Jade's pale, drawn face was enough to convince him that she'd reached the end of her tether.

"You're tired," she persisted. "I can take over for a while."

"Long hours are part of my job." But added to the way his head was splitting, he suspected his fatigue would soon reach a dangerous state. "It can't be more than a couple of miles farther, if that. Once you're safely settled, I'll use Stan's landline to call Jackson. Maybe then I can crash for a couple of hours."

She let out a breath, audible in the close confines of the truck's cab. "I can hardly believe it's almost over."

"It is." He grasped her hand for a quick squeeze, all her could risk at the moment. "We're going to get through this."

They would. This day had been like running a 10K, sure at times he'd never make it, reduced to just putting one foot in front of the other. Then, suddenly, the finish line would loom ahead, small in the distance but getting bigger with every step. That's where they were now, with the finish line almost in sight.

The truck veered a bit to the left, and he steadied it, peering ahead in the gathering dusk. "There—is that a signpost on the right?"

Jade leaned forward, her face a pale oval in the dim light. "Mountaintop Lodge. That's it!"

A spurt of energy surged through him. "I told you we'd make it." He patted the steering wheel as if it were the shoulder of his favorite horse. "I knew this old girl wouldn't let us down."

Jade swung toward him. "You will see that it gets back

to Mamie Carson, won't you? And I'd like to give her a thank-you gift." She smiled, the sight lifting his spirits. "I suppose a flower arrangement isn't really a sensible gift in the middle of winter."

"We'll get the truck back safely, with a full tank of gas. Let me think about the gift. I'm sure we can find something she can use."

We. Using the word to refer to the two of them pleased him. There'd be plenty of future occasions when they'd be buying gifts together, making plans together, doing all the things a couple did. His mother was going to love Jade. She'd start dreaming of grandchildren the minute she knew he'd found someone.

The lane to the lodge had recently been plowed. They rounded a curve and there the lodge was, settled into the mountain as if it had grown there, its rough-hewn timbers blending into the surrounding woods.

"Stan's got a light on for us." He drew up to the wide porch and stopped. "With a little luck, he has a pot of soup on the range."

He slid out. A wave of dizziness hit when his feet touched the ground. He grabbed the door to keep from falling.

Jade was out and around the car in an instant, supporting him. "You need a doctor." Her tone, worried and scolding all at once, comforted him.

Suck it up, he ordered himself as he straightened. "I'm okay." He slammed the truck door by way of emphasis. "Let's get inside."

Arms around each other, they stumbled up the three steps to the porch. The front door swept open, revealing Stan's bulgy, balding figure standing in a rectangle of golden light.

"Micah! Good to see you, good to see you. And your friend. Come in here and warm up."

He gestured them inside, his round face beaming. "I was beginning to think you got lost. Shouldn't take you that long to get here from Billings."

"We had a few detours," Micah said dryly.

Warmth surrounded them the instant they stepped into the high-ceilinged lobby. A fire burned in the stone fireplace, welcoming them.

Jade took a step away from him, as if she'd suddenly realized that they were clinging together. "This is beautiful, Mr...." She broke off, apparently realizing she didn't know his name.

"Just call me Stan, Ms. Summers. Glad you like it. Don't you worry about a thing. You'll be safe here. Just come on in, take your jackets off, relax. Nothing to worry about now that you're here."

It took concentrated thought to pull off his gloves, unzip his jacket. He'd gotten it halfway off when he was aware of a faint warning alarm going off in the back of his fatigue-fogged brain.

Ms. Summers, Stan had said. But he hadn't told Stan who he was bringing. He'd never mentioned a name. He was sure of that. It was second nature.

He let the heavy parka drop to the floor, kicking it out of his way as he reached for Jade with one hand and his weapon with the other.

"Jade..."

She turned toward him at the sound of her name, her eyes widening at his expression. Stan turned, too. His face was a ludicrous combination of joviality and guilt.

"Micah, what's goin' on? You don't need a gun in here."

"Maybe I do." If he was wrong, he'd apologize, but he'd err on the side of caution. He pulled Jade behind him. "How did you know Ms. Summers's name, Stan?"

"You told me, man. That's all. You told me."

"I don't think so." He forced his brain to function, going over that phone conversation which felt as if it had happened in another decade.

"Sure you did." Stan's grin widened. "Listen, you know you can trust me. Hey, I owe you my life. You think I'd forget that."

"Micah?"

At the sound of Jade's questioning voice, his mind cleared. He was right. And that meant that Stan...

"He's figured it out, Stan."

Micah swiveled. A man stood in the door to Stan's office, his dark suit an incongruous detail in this setting. He held a businesslike automatic in his hand, and it was pointed straight at Jade's heart.

A shudder swept through Jade, as cold and paralyzing as if she'd been doused with ice water. Betrayal. They'd been betrayed. Micah's friend had betrayed them.

"You're keeping strange company, aren't you, Stan? What's Frankie Como doing here?" Micah's voice was cold, too. One hand reached toward her.

She made an instinctive movement toward that hand, but the man...Como...Micah had said, gave a warning sound.

"Just stay perfectly still, Ms. Summers. Let's not do anything we'll regret." His tone was cultured, almost pleasant, as if he really regretted the unfortunate events that had brought them to this.

"Stan's already done something to regret." If Micah

felt pain at this betrayal, he covered it. "What was it, Stan? How did they get to you?"

Stan backed up a step, shrugging. "Guess maybe I wasn't really cut out for living way up here, hardly seeing a soul. It was tough to break all the old ties. You oughta know that." He shrugged. "So, I stayed in touch. I hear things. Like how much money Vincent Martino has out on some woman he wants iced. I wouldna done nothing about it, but when you called, it just seemed like it was meant."

Como lifted his shoulders slightly. "Stan, Stan. Your tongue is running away with you. Somebody might have to do something about that."

Stan blanched. "Sorry. I didn't mean…" He mumbled off into silence.

"So, what's Vincent Martino's right-hand man doing getting mixed up in this?"

Micah's weight shifted slightly as he said the words. Jade, attuned to his every movement, sensed it. He was going to do something. She had to be ready to help him, but what could she do?

Como frowned. "Too many errors have been occurring. I told Vincent myself that his actions were unwise, but he didn't listen. Now it's left to me to clean up all his loose ends. So I came myself, along with a couple of pros."

"You should have made sure your pros knew how to drive on icy roads," Micah said.

"True, they erred," Como admitted. "But they did catch up with you eventually. After all, we knew where you were going. They got just close enough to make sure you headed up here."

A fresh chill went down her spine. He'd known all along where they were, waiting here like a spider in a web. Como's idea of cleaning up matters probably meant leaving no witnesses.

Ahead of her, slightly to the left, an oval table bore a brass lamp. A nice, heavy, brass lamp.

"Stand still, Marshal." Como snapped the words. "Let the gun fall to the floor, and then kick it over toward Stan."

Micah obeyed, held prisoner by the fact that the man still had his weapon trained on her. But the distraction provided by his actions gave her an instant to ease a step nearer the table, her heart hammering so loudly she feared he could hear it.

Don't give up, she ordered herself. *Don't you dare give up.*

Yea, though I walk through the valley of the shadow of death, Thou art with me…

Be with us, Lord. Protect us. Give me courage to act when I have to.

Micah straightened, and the moment's respite was over. Stan held Micah's gun, a trace of uneasiness on his face. Maybe he hadn't minded betraying his friend in the abstract, but now that he was face-to-face with him, it was different. That could give them a little edge, couldn't it?

Please, God. Touch whatever conscience that man has left.

"Hold the weapon on Marshal McGraw." Como snapped the order. "Ms. Summers, step toward me."

Micah made an instinctive move.

"Don't be foolish, McGraw." Como almost sounded tired of this. "I just want to have a better look at her. Come into the light, Ms. Summers."

She moved forward. Every step took her farther from

Micah, and that was a physical pain, as if she separated from herself.

But it gave Micah a little more of a chance, didn't it? And brought her closer to the only potential weapon she might get her hands on.

She'd never hit anyone, not in her whole life. But she could do it, if it meant her life or Micah's.

Como moved closer to her, close enough that she caught a whiff of some expensive scent. The barrel of his gun pointed at her chest, unwavering, while he leaned nearer, seeming to study her lips. He touched her chin, his fingers cold, tilting it toward the light. Her skin crawling, she had to force herself not to cringe away.

Micah hated the man touching her. She sensed his anger and clung to it, taking strength from that to remain still.

Finally Como moved back, shaking his head.

"Too bad," he said. "After all this trouble, she's not the right one, either. I told Vincent he was going about this all wrong, but he wouldn't listen."

"I don't know what you're talking about." She burst into speech, hoping to keep his attention on her long enough for Micah to act. "Wrong one? What does that even mean? Why have you been chasing us?"

He smiled thinly. "That doesn't really matter now, Ms. Summers. Right one or wrong one, you two got too close to the family. So now, I'm afraid you have to die."

SIXTEEN

He had to move, now. Rush Como, take a chance that Stan wouldn't fire, that Como wouldn't put a bullet in Jade before he could reach her...

"Wait a minute." Stan turned to Como, the weapon sagging in his hand. "Nobody said anything about killing people in my place. I'm not gonna get involved in killing a fed."

"Don't be such a fool. You knew why we were here." Como sounded contemptuous. "Don't try to salve your conscience now, when we all know you don't have one."

Stan took a step back, shaking his head. The gun pointed at the floor. "I'm not gonna get involved in killing a fed," he repeated.

"Shut up." Como's smile tightened against his teeth until his face looked like a death mask. "You'll do as you're told, you idiot." For an instant, his gaze moved to Stan.

Long enough. Micah charged toward the man, brushing past Jade, praying she had enough sense to run for the door, buy another moment of life. Como's gun went off. Hot pain pierced his shoulder. He kept going, charging into the man, knocking his arm up so that the shots went wildly toward the ceiling.

"Jade, run!"

He thought he shouted the words, but he couldn't be sure. All he could do was cling to Como's arm, knowing that the instant he let go he'd be a dead man. Knowing that the strength was draining out of him, he couldn't hold on much longer, he had to, had to, Jade's life, his life…

Movement next to him. A resounding crash. And Como slumped to the floor like a sack of grain.

"Jade…" He managed to say her name. Jade, the remains of a lamp still clutched in her hands, holding his life there.

His legs wouldn't hold him up. He crumpled, feeling Como's limp body beneath him as he fell.

He had to hang on. He blinked, trying to focus his eyes. Couldn't black out and leave Jade to deal with this on her own.

"Cuffs," he muttered. "In my pocket. Cuff him." He tried to raise his head, but it was too heavy. "Where's Stan?"

"He ran out." Jade's arms went around him. "You're bleeding. Micah…" Her voice broke on his name, and he knew she was crying.

"Hang on." He forced strength he didn't feel into his voice. "I'm okay. Cuff him. Get the weapons." It would be too easy to shut his eyes, to lapse into the darkness that pulled at him. "Do it."

"Yes. Right." She moved, letting go.

He slumped back, rolling off Como, watching as she handcuffed him. She seemed reluctant to touch him, but she did it.

Gingerly, she searched him for weapons, pulling a second gun out of the holster on Como's leg. She collected Micah's gun, too, that Stan had dropped in his eagerness to get out. She moved them safely out of Como's reach. Then she came to him, dropping onto her knees and putting her arms around him.

"Got to find a phone," he muttered. "Call for help…"

"I will. I'll call." She drew his head against her shoulder, her arms cradling him. Her hair caressed his face, and her tears wet his skin.

"I love you." It was the faintest whisper, so faint maybe he was imagining it.

For the moment they were safe. *Thank You, God.* He slid into blackness.

"Listen, I've got to get out of here. I'm fine. Now give me my clothes."

The nurse who'd been taking his blood pressure looked unimpressed. "You'll leave the hospital when the doctor says, and not a moment before."

"He giving you trouble, nurse?" Jackson stood in the doorway, looking remarkably fresh given the fact that he probably hadn't slept in forty-eight hours.

"Nothing I can't handle," she said. She checked his IV, twitched at the sheet and marched out of the room.

"What's going on?" Micah demanded. He had only the haziest memory of what happened after he passed out. "Where's Jade? Is she all right? What about Como? And Stan?"

Jackson let the door swing shut behind him and advanced on the bed. "You lay back and quit straining that shoulder, and I'll answer all your questions. If not, that nurse will come back and kick me out."

"Jade," he said, and there was pleading in his voice. He'd undoubtedly have to endure one of Jackson's biting lectures on his behavior, but first he had to know she was all right.

"She's fine." Jackson's granite jaw actually relaxed a little. "She's quite a tiger, you know that?"

He knew. That strange pang in his heart at the mention of her name had to be love.

"When we got to the lodge, the cavalry riding to the rescue after your call, we found Como trussed up like a Thanksgiving turkey and you with your head on a pillow, your shoulder bandaged, all tucked up in blankets."

He managed a smile at the implied criticism. "Should have been the other way around."

"Not to hear Ms. Summers tell it. She says you took a bullet to save her."

"Taking the bullet was my job. Did she tell you she hit Como over the head with a lamp when I was on the verge of passing out? Otherwise, you'd be planning a funeral today."

"So you saved each other." Jackson's face tightened at the mention of a funeral, but he didn't show any other emotion. "Nothing wrong with that."

Micah spoke the question that was haunting him. "Where is she?"

If the powers that be made Jade disappear into Witness Protection, leaving behind all she loved, then he'd still have failed her.

"She's here, in Billings. Fact is, she's right here in the hospital, waiting for me to talk to you first."

His heart seemed to swell. "You're not going to move her?"

"There doesn't seem much need." Jackson sat down gingerly on the edge of the bed. "Como's being a good soldier and not talking, but we caught up with Stan, and he's babbling like a brook. He confirmed what we already suspected—that Vincent Martino is out to find Eloise and kill her as some kind of twisted tribute to his dying father."

Jackson didn't betray much emotion, ever. But Micah knew him well enough to detect the feelings that roiled in him when he talked about the threat to Eloise. Or maybe his newfound feelings for Jade had made him more sensitive to others.

"You care about her," Micah said quietly.

Jackson's jaw clenched. He wasn't going to respond. Well, not surprising. They didn't have that kind of relationship.

"I care about her," Jackson said slowly. "I let her down once. I won't do that again."

"I'm sorry." Micah reached out.

His brother took his hand. Clasped it tightly. Then let it drop as he turned away.

For a moment there was silence. Then Jackson cleared his throat.

"That reminds me. Now that we know just what we're up against, I'm putting together a task force to work the whole case. People I know I can trust."

Micah's mind winced away from the thought of the traitor among the people he knew. "That's good."

"Fact is, I need one more person." Jackson lifted an eyebrow at him. "What about it?"

Micah could only stare at him. "You mean me?"

"Who else? Your chief approves, but it's going to be hush-hush otherwise. We don't want to alert the leak before we're ready to pounce on him. So, what do you say?"

"You bet." He couldn't stop the grin that spread over his face.

"Good. There's plenty to do. We'll pull in every favor

owed us, tag every snitch. Fact is, I got a tip from a Chicago cop, a guy named Clay West. He used to be a friend of Eloise. He says there's a nosy Montana reporter who's trying to tie the deaths out here to Witness Protection. We'll have to see how she got on to something that shouldn't be known outside the department."

"I know some people at the paper…" Micah lost his train of thought when the door swung open. It was Jade.

Jade hesitated, her hand bracing the swinging door to the patient room. Jackson and Micah turned in unison to look at her.

How alike they were—both men of intense integrity, with a certain steel in them that had been tried and found strong. Did they even realize what they shared?

"I can come back if you aren't finished," she said it tentatively, not wanting to break in on official business. Maybe even not quite ready to talk to Micah just yet.

"No, come in." Jackson waved her into the room, stepping back from the bed to make room for her. "I was just telling Micah that you should be in the clear now."

"That's good to hear." It was all she'd been hoping for, but now her mind and heart were completely filled with Micah. With what she had to say to him.

"Martino knows you're not the one he's looking for," Jackson said. "And we've let it be known that Como is being charged for the assault on a federal officer. Word has it that Martino is so annoyed with Como for fouling up that he's cut him loose."

"Any chance Como will flip on him, in that case?" Micah had on his cop's face, watchful and intent.

"So far he's being the good soldier, but we'll keep the

pressure on." Jackson patted Micah's good arm and then walked quickly to the door. "I'll be in touch. Meantime…" A smile touched his face. "You two take care of each other."

The door swung shut behind him. The still room seemed to hold its breath.

She had to say the things she'd been planning when she'd walked in the room. They'd both been in an emotional pressure cooker for days. She couldn't let that push Micah into thinking he had feelings for her that weren't real. She couldn't…

His fingers closed over her hand then, robbing her of rational thought. He pulled her down to sit on the bed next to him.

"What's going on?" His voice was gentle. "Are you okay?"

"I'm fine." She looked down at their hands because she couldn't look at his face. But that was almost worse, because his strong, tanned fingers intertwined with hers, making her feel a part of him.

She took a breath, trying to get it past the lump in her throat. She had to do this.

"I…I just wanted to say… Well, last night, things were a little crazy."

That was putting it mildly. She'd been terrified that Micah would bleed to death in her arms, unable to think, just able to hold him and pray frantically.

Suddenly the door had burst open, and FBI agents had stormed in, terrifying her all over again with their weapons. They'd taken over, hauling Como, still unconscious or faking it, away from her. They'd pulled her away from Micah, firing questions at her.

But then Jackson had come. His face, when he looked at his brother...

Before she knew it, she and Micah were in a helicopter, bound for the hospital in Billings.

"I don't remember much of it," he said. "Just my brother, snapping orders at everyone. And then being in a chopper, with you holding my hand."

She felt a flush mount in her cheeks. "Yes, well..."

"Of course I also seem to remember that you saved my life."

That made it worse. She couldn't let him imagine feelings for her because he thought he owed her for knocking out Como.

"I...I might have said something that I—"

Her words were cut off by Micah's hand, warm across her lips.

"Don't. Don't even try to deny what you said. You said you loved me."

"Yes," she whispered, not looking at him.

"That's a good thing, because I feel the same way."

She shook her head, freeing her lips. "You don't have to say that. I don't want to push you into something you're not ready for."

He gave her a rueful grin. "Funny. That's just what I was thinking about you. That I had to go slow, give you time, let you get to know me under normal circumstances."

"That's right." She seized on his words. "That's what we should do."

"But I don't want to." He cupped her cheek in his hand, and his warmth and tenderness seemed to flood through her.

"We...we should take it slow. I mean, logically speaking, we've only known each other for a couple of weeks."

His thumb brushed across her lips, hushing her. "Let's set logic aside for the moment. You can learn a lot about someone in a couple of weeks like these. You can learn something about yourself, too."

Her gaze met his, and she felt herself drowning in their chocolate depths. "What did you learn about yourself?" She wasn't quite brave enough to ask what he'd learned about her.

"You know, I've always tried to play down my instincts. Figured that I'd be a better officer if I didn't rely on feelings, just facts." His thumb caressed her lips again. "But my instincts were right on target where you were concerned. And I think they saved our lives last night. So I'm not going to worry so much about that keeping me from being the officer I was meant to be."

She closed her hand around his wrist, and his pulse throbbed against her hand, seeming to give her strength.

"I'm glad. Glad you're sure now of who you are. And so thankful you've been there with me. If not for you, I might not have found my way back to God."

His breath caught, and his eyes filled with tears. Then he shook his head. "Don't give me the credit. God was never going to let you go, Jade. The lousy parents you had don't matter in the long run. You're His child."

"I know." She blinked back tears.

"And if you're about to say something else about waiting, you can save your breath." His hand slid up under her hair, cradling her head. "I'm not going to argue with God's timing."

All her doubts lifted away like mist from the mountains. Micah was right. Through all the dark times, through all the terror, God had been with her, holding her hand. He'd brought her through the darkness into the light and given her someone to love. She couldn't deny that.

And then she couldn't think at all, because Micah drew her down to capture her lips with his in a kiss so strong and sweet that it sealed everything they were to each other. Forever.

* * * * *

Dear Reader,

I'm so glad you decided to pick up the first book in our exciting new continuity series from Love Inspired Suspense. It's been such a pleasure to work with five such talented authors on creating these continuing stories. I hope you'll check back every month through June to pick up another installment.

The love story of Jade and Micah touched my heart as I wrote, and I hope you'll find that it touches yours. I love writing about the relationship between two people who find that they complement each other perfectly, in the way God has planned for them.

I hope you'll let me know how you felt about this story, and I'd love to send you a signed bookmark or my brochure of Pennsylvania Dutch recipes. You can write to me at Steeple Hill Books, 233 Broadway, Suite 1001, New York, NY 10279, e-mail me at: marta@martaperry.com, or visit me on the Web at: www.martaperry.com.

Blessings,

Marta Perry

QUESTIONS FOR DISCUSSION

1. Can you understand the difficulty Jade experienced in starting a new life in Montana? Have you ever struggled to deal with a major life change like this? If so, how did God and other people help you with it?

2. Jade's grief at the loss of her sister is complicated by the threat to her and by her own sense of guilt. Did you empathize with her?

3. Jade had drifted away from God at a time when she felt God didn't hear her. Has this every happened to you? How did you deal with it?

4. Micah struggles with the conflict he sees between his duties as a lawman and his natural empathy for Jade. Did you understand his struggle between duty and love?

5. The depth of her grief over her sister's death eventually brings Jade back to God. Have you ever experienced something that suddenly made you aware of your need for God?

6. The scripture verse for this story was the first one I memorized as a child, and it never fails to give me strength, particularly the hymn setting for the Psalm that I mention in the story. Do you have a verse that gives you strength in this way?

7. Micah feels he has to choose between his instincts and following the rules in order to protect Jade. Did you understand his actions? Do you think he was right?

8. Jade is touched by the unselfish actions of a perfect stranger when Ms. Carson rescues them in the storm. Have you ever experienced that? Do you feel that God sent someone to you, or that God sent you to be "a raven" to someone else?

9. Because of the chaos of her early life, Jade needed order and permanence surrounding her. Did that make her more vulnerable to the stresses of finding life out of her control? How do you think she coped with that?

10. Did you sympathize with the life Jade wanted to create for herself when she moved to Montana? How do our surroundings give us a sense of peace?

11. Micah compared himself to his older brother and his father and felt he was lacking. Is there anyone in your life you look up to in that way? Is it possible to look up to someone without making yourself feel less worthy in comparison?

12. Which character in the story did you feel exemplified Christlike behavior? Why?

13. What did it take to bring Jade to the point that she could trust enough to love?

14. Did you end the book feeling eager to read the next installment in the series?

*Now that Jade is safe, who will be the Mob's next
target? Newspaper reporter Violet Kramer is
determined to find out before someone else dies.
But is she putting her own life in danger
by going after the story?*

*Read on for a sneak preview of
KILLER HEADLINE by Debby Giusti,
the second exciting book in the
PROTECTING THE WITNESSES series,
available February 2010
from Love Inspired Suspense.*

Violet Kramer looked up from her laptop, relieved the
drapes were drawn and the doors locked. Her attention
was focused on her computer screen and the information
she'd compiled over the last few weeks.

Violet could smell a good story, and this one was as
strong as Limburger cheese. Not that she had all the
threads that would eventually weave together a front-
page spread, but she had enough to keep her digging
until she uncovered the bits and pieces that would turn
a great beginning into a great headliner, sure to improve her current odd-man-out status at the *Missoula
Daily News.*

Even more important, the story would warn other
women who might be in danger. Women who had somehow tangled with organized crime. Like Ruby Summers
Maxwell and Carlie Donald, both murdered in Montana.

Both young and attractive with the dubious distinction of having testified against the Mob.

Another interesting similarity, both women had green eyes. An important clue or coincidence? Violet wasn't sure.

She had little to go on concerning Ruby's death, except an e-mail from a reporter friend who worked on the local rag in the town where Ruby had been killed. The story had never appeared in print: women in the Witness Protection Program didn't get obits in the morning news.

Luckily, Violet's diligent search of area newspapers had paid off with a photo of Jade Summers—the very-much-alive twin sister of the murder victim—standing next to her beau, Deputy U.S. Marshal Micah McGraw. At least now Violet knew what Jade's murdered twin had looked like.

From the reticence on the part of the police in both Montana towns, Ruby's and Carlie's deaths seemed to have gone almost unnoticed, like those of too many other people who mixed with the Mob. Violet should know: she'd been studying the Mafia's heinous activity since her Chicago internship.

Closing her eyes, Violet tried to block out all the gory details of the case playing through her mind. Her day had started early with a long run before church. She had spent the afternoon working on the information about the murders, which had stretched the long day into an even longer night. A lot of people believed deaths came in threes. So who would be the next to die? If the police couldn't figure it out, Violet would.

* * * * *

*Will Violet's nose for news put her on the Mob's
radar or can a handsome Chicago cop
prevent her from digging too far?*

*To find out pick up
KILLER HEADLINE by Debby Giusti,
available in February 2010
from Love Inspired Suspense.*

LARGER-PRINT BOOKS!

**GET 2 FREE
LARGER-PRINT NOVELS
PLUS 2 FREE
MYSTERY GIFTS**

Love Inspired.
SUSPENSE
RIVETING INSPIRATIONAL ROMANCE

Larger-print novels are now available...

LISUSLP10

Love Inspired

Newspaper reporter Amanda Bodine's boss keeps assigning her fluff pieces about dog shows and boat parades. She longs to prove herself to Ross Lockhart with a serious front-page story. Until her own family becomes newsworthy…

Look for

Heart of the Matter
by
Marta Perry

the
**Bodine
Family**

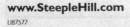